"Why pry into my private life, Max?"

Max smiled and replied easily, "I like to know what makes people tick."

"What if I said that, with my husband dead, I've decided not to fall in love again. Perhaps I've decided to have an affair in every town. You men do that sort of thing—why shouldn't a woman?"

Max's smile hardened. "How interesting," he said, reaching for her hand. "We have something in common, after all. Because, you see, ever since I walked into your hotel room, I've wanted you."

This wasn't what she'd wanted to accomplish at all. Her panic rising, she snatched her fingers from his grip. "I don't find that humorous. Or flattering."

Max laughed. "I didn't think you would. Take my advice, Whitney. Stay out of poker games—you're lousy at bluffs."

LEIGH MICHAELS likes writing romance fiction spiced with humor and a dash of suspense and adventure. She holds a degree in journalism and teaches creative writing in Iowa. She and her husband, a photographer, have two children but include in their family a dog-pound mutt who thinks he's human and a Siamese "aristo-cat," both of whom have appeared in her books. When asked if her husband and children have also been characterized, the author pleads the Fifth Amendment.

Books by Leigh Michaels

HARLEQUIN PRESENTS
876—TOUCH NOT MY HEART
900—LEAVING HOME
1004—THE GRAND HOTEL
1028—BRITTANY'S CASTLE
1049—CARLISLE PRIDE
1068—REBEL WITH A CAUSE
1107—CLOSE COLLABORATION

HARLEQUIN ROMANCE
2657—ON SEPTEMBER HILL
2734—WEDNESDAY'S CHILD
2748—COME NEXT SUMMER
2806—CAPTURE A SHADOW
2830—O'HARA'S LEGACY
2879—SELL ME A DREAM
2951—STRICTLY BUSINESS

Don't miss any of our special offers. Write to us at the following address for information on our newest releases.

Harlequin Reader Service
901 Fuhrmann Blvd., P.O. Box 1397, Buffalo, NY 14240
Canadian address: P.O. Box 603,
Fort Erie, Ont. L2A 5X3

LEIGH MICHAELS

a new desire

Harlequin Books

TORONTO • NEW YORK • LONDON
AMSTERDAM • PARIS • SYDNEY • HAMBURG
STOCKHOLM • ATHENS • TOKYO • MILAN

For Arnie and Laural—
with love and thanks
(Have I got a deal for you!)

Harlequin Presents first edition February 1989
ISBN 0-373-11147-9

Original hardcover edition published in 1988
by Mills & Boon Limited

CHAPTER ONE

WHITNEY shook her head at the skycap who offered to take her luggage; her single leather bag had wheels on it, and she had learned in years of flying never to let go of the matching carry-on that held her emergency supplies. She looked at her watch and wanted to swear. The delay in Customs hadn't been the problem; it had been brief. And they had left Tokyo right on time. It was the long, unscheduled layover in Alaska to check out some mysterious malfunction in the monster aircraft's engines that had landed her in a predicament. If it hadn't been for that stupid aeroplane, she wouldn't have missed her connection with the flight that should have taken her on home.

She yawned, and shook her head wearily. All she wanted right now was to open the door of her own apartment and creep wearily into her own bed to recuperate from jet-lag and exhaustion.

But that was only an idealistic dream, she reminded herself. Even if she could get home, the apartment wouldn't be entirely calm. There would be two weeks' worth of mail to cope with, and the telephone would probably be ringing off the wall. Ross always knew the instant she walked in, and he would want an immediate report on her trip. He had some sort of sixth sense where she was concerned, Whitney thought. It was one of the disadvantages in working so closely with her brother.

I've got the answer, she thought. I'll just check into a hotel here and sleep for a couple of days, and then go on home.

It was a tempting idea, but she pushed it aside and walked on towards the airline desk to see what they could do about her ticket to Chicago—a useless scrap of paper now that the jetliner she should have been on was thirty thousand feet in the air, speeding eastward, somewhere over Denver by now.

A mechanical voice crackled over the public address system. 'Whitney Lattimer, call the operator, please. Whitney Lattimer, call the operator.'

Dammit, she thought. He couldn't even wait till I was home! She found a house phone.

The operator's crisp, clear, voice warmed into pleasantness. 'We've been paging you off and on for hours, Mrs Lattimer.'

'Sorry,' Whitney said crisply. 'I couldn't hear you in Anchorage, I'm afraid.' She didn't need to jot down the number the operator gave; she had learned it by heart long ago. It was the private number that rang into Ross's office.

The telephone was snatched up as soon as it started to ring. 'Well, that's flattering,' Whitney said. 'Have you been sitting there all day waiting for me to call?'

'Where in hell have you been?' There was undeniable anxiety in her brother's voice, and Whitney could picture him at his desk, bracing one hand on the edge of it. He had really been worried about her, she thought, and a trickle of pleasure warmed her.

'Having engine trouble in Alaska,' she said. 'Didn't you bother to check with the airline?'

'What was wrong with the engine?'

'How should I know? They never tell the passengers. Perhaps the mechanics in Tokyo forgot to change the spark plugs or something.'

'Jets don't have 'em.'

'Why does it matter, anyway? I don't have the vaguest idea what the problem was. I only know that I'm hours late. Did you want me to call just so we could chat about the airline's equipment?'

'Not exactly.'

'Well, if you want a report on my trip, I'd much rather wait till I'm back in the store tomorrow.'

'Tomorrow is what I want to talk to you about.'

'That makes two of us,' Whitney said. 'I missed my connection, so I'm going to stay overnight and come back to Chicago tomorrow. All right?'

'Not all right. I need you in Kansas City in the morning.'

Whitney's hand clenched on the telephone. 'If this is your idea of a joke, Ross——'

'Unfortunately, it's not. Max Townsend's spent the last two weeks studying the problems in the Kansas City store, and he needs one of us there tomorrow so he can make his report.'

'If it has taken two weeks already, can't it wait another day or two?'

'Max says it's too important to be put off.'

'Then why not make him come to Chicago?'

'He can't bring the evidence here.'

'Well, Max Townsend is your treasure, not mine, Ross. It's got nothing to do with me.'

'You are still a vice-president of this corporation. Besides——' his voice tightened '—you owe me one, Whitney, and you know it.'

Whitney smothered the urge to click her heels together and salute. If she had been face to face with him, she would have done it, she swore. Ross could be an inconsiderate swine at times.

But this time, he was right, the little voice at the back of her brain reminded her. Ross could also be the world's most thoughtful brother, and to tell the truth, she owed him a great deal more than one favour. But not today! she protested to herself. Today, she just wanted to sleep.

'Can't it wait?' she pleaded.

'Max says not.'

'Max says,' she repeated irritably. 'Really, Ross, it sounds as if you've abdicated all responsibility for the entire chain of stores. It seems that Max is suddenly the one with all the power.'

'Max knows what he's talking about, Whitney.'

'How can he? He's never even worked for a department store.'

'He was right about the problems in Lake Forest.'

'That, my dear brother, was a lucky guess. And what the Lake Forest store has to do with Kansas City is beyond me. There is nothing wrong with the Kansas City store beyond the fact that it's only six months old. Whatever problems it has, it will outgrow. I never thought it was necessary to send an efficiency expert in.'

'Max is not an efficiency expert. He's a management consultant, and a damned good one.' There was a brief silence. Then he said, in a softer tone, 'Look, Whitney, I know how you feel about Max.'

'Not just Max,' she interrupted. 'I dislike efficiency experts. Oh, all right, if you insist—management consultants in general.'

'That's why I've never asked you to work with him before, and I wouldn't ask now if I didn't have to. I'd love to go down there myself to see what he's found, but I'm thoroughly stuck here for at least the next ten days. Whit, please.'

From the days of their childhood, whenever Ross said, 'Whit, please,' in just that tone of voice, Whitney had melted.

'All right!' she said irritably. 'I'll see if I can get a flight first thing in the morning.'

'I've already arranged it,' Ross said. 'There's a direct flight to Kansas City leaving in less than an hour. You can pick up your ticket at——'

'Dammit, Ross! If I had any sense at all I'd hang up on you. If I hadn't been so blasted tired I'd have ignored that page altogether.'

'I told you a long time ago to learn to sleep on aeroplanes.'

Whitney ignored him. 'I should have known as soon as they called my name that you were up to no good!'

'There's no hurry on the Tokyo report,' he added comfortably. 'Let's get Kansas City straightened out first. It's only the middle of the afternoon now.'

'Ross,' she said, keeping her voice level with an effort, 'It may be the middle of the afternoon here, but I'm still on Tokyo time. On top of that, I spent eight hours in Anchorage waiting for them to work on those damned engines——'

'They might have been changing the oil,' Ross said mildly. 'Or do jets have oil?'

'I don't care if they were putting in tomato juice! I'm trying to tell you that I've already been up since tomorrow!'

'Don't you mean yesterday?'

'No. Maybe. I never did understand the International Date Line. I don't know what I mean, except that I will not go to Kansas City today.'

'Max wants to meet you first thing in the morning.'

'Max the Magnificent can wait!'

'Whitney, you've never even met the man. You didn't see him work in Lake Forest——'

'I've heard plenty about him, and I'm not impressed. If you want somebody in Kansas City tomorrow morning, Ross, it will have to be you. Have a good time.' She put the phone down with a bang. But she didn't leave the booth. She smoothed the uncrushable fabric of her suit and wished idly that the principles of polyester could be applied to people too.

Max Townsend was the only person she knew who could give Ross orders, she thought. Her parting jab had been closer to truth than she had planned; if Max wanted a company executive in Kansas City tomorrow morning, there would be one. If Whitney refused, Ross would go.

And he wouldn't fuss about it. He was too good an executive to use personal pressure, even when the reluctant employee was his own sister. Ross could have reminded her—but he hadn't—that the reason he didn't want to leave Chicago just now was that his first child was due to be born any day.

He didn't have to remind me, she thought. He was smart enough to know that I'd remember it myself, and that I'd feel unbearably guilty if my brother had to leave his wife right now because I didn't want to follow orders.

Ross had been the best of brothers, she reminded herself. In the awful months after Whitney's husband had died, when she had been trying to cope with the guilt, Ross had always been there, whenever she had needed his help or his reassuring presence or just his broad shoulder to cry on. Now, he needed her, and she owed him one.

Whitney picked up the telephone again and punched the number irritably, hurrying so that she couldn't think it over and change her mind. When Ross answered, she said wearily, 'All right. You and Max win. Where do I pick up my ticket?'

It was rush-hour by the time her cab reached downtown Kansas City. Despite the fact that the freeways were bumper to bumper, traffic was moving at a frantic pace. She watched with detached interest as the driver cut into a space that was at least an inch longer than the cab itself. 'Is traffic always this bad?' she asked.

'Not usually. There's a convention going on downtown, so there are a lot more cars. Tourists!' he muttered, jamming on the brakes as the car in front slowed abruptly. The cab skidded into the next lane, and the cabbie smiled at Whitney in the mirror. 'And the highway work always slows everything down.'

'This is slow?' She could see the speedometer.

'Dreadful. Which hotel did you say?'

'Henry the Eighth—near Country Club Plaza.'

'Oh, yes. Isn't that the one with the funny slogan?'

'"At Henry the Eighth, a man's hotel is really his castle"? That's the one.'

The cabbie laughed appreciatively. 'You here for the convention?'

'No. Business.' She grabbed for a handhold as the cab swung off the freeway. 'Would you drive through Country Club Plaza on the way to the hotel?'

'Fine with me. Do you want the whole tour?'

'No. Just drive past the Tyler-Royale department store.' At least she could see if Max Townsend had left the place standing.

'You work for them or something?'

'That's right.'

'Oh.' There was sympathy in the cabbie's tone. He negotiated traffic in silence for a few minutes, and then added, 'Too bad.'

Whitney gave him a quizzical look, but before she could ask what he meant, her attention was distracted by the sight of the store itself. The Tyler-Royale store was small by the chain's standards, three stories of sand-coloured brick, trimmed with the bright mosaic tile borders that accented the entire small shopping district. The store looked the same as it had at the Grand Opening ceremonies last spring, Whitney thought. From the outside, it certainly didn't appear to be a store in trouble. There were shoppers going in, coming out, walking past.

She turned her attention back to the cabbie as the vehicle negotiated a sharp turn. 'What did you mean, too bad?'

'That store's a loser. Darn shame, too.' The cab screeched to a halt under the canopy at the hotel entrance. 'Here you go, Your Majesty—Henry the Eighth!' He was laughing at his own joke.

Whitney would have liked to ask him why he had assessed the new store as a failure. Then she chided herself. What did a cabbie know about retail merchandising, anyway?

She paid him and went thoughtfully on into the lobby of the hotel, all stone and timbers and heavy beams like the great hall of a castle. It was well done, Whitney thought; in looking at it, one could almost forget that the beams were plastic reproductions and the stone had been artistically moulded on the spot.

The registration desk was busy. She waited patiently, glad that Tyler-Royale had made arrangements even before the store opened for a suite to be permanently kept available for visiting executives and dignitaries.

People like Max Townsend. Why hadn't she thought of that earlier, Whitney wondered in exhausted irritation. If Max was staying in the suite, then where on earth—in a town crowded with conventioneers—would she find a place to sleep?

Before she had a chance to think about this startling bit of conjecture, the desk clerk looked up with a smile. 'Do you have a reservation?' she asked.

'Not exactly. I'm Whitney Lattimer of Tyler-Royale.'

'Oh, yes. I'll still need you to sign in, though, so the desk can get your phone calls straight.'

I hope there aren't any, Whitney thought. She signed the card and asked, hesitantly, 'There isn't anyone else staying there already, is there?'

'In the suite? No, ma'am. All the keys are here.' The clerk looked a little blank.

Thank heaven, Whitney thought. 'Our staff comes in and out all the time,' she said lightly. 'I never quite know who I might run into.'

The clerk said, 'Yes, ma'am,' but it was obvious that she was already more concerned about the next person on line.

The bellboy showed her up in the crowded lift. He checked the small living-room, the kitchenette, the bedroom, the bath. He turned on the lights, arranged her luggage, pulled the curtains wide. Then he pocketed the tip and cheerfully vanished. Whitney kicked off her shoes and ran her fingers through her hair, smiling at herself. 'Maybe you should have made him look in the cupboards,' she jeered aloud. 'After all, Max might be hiding there, waiting to jump out at you——'

Max, she thought, had probably demanded accommodation more to his liking. The Henry the Eighth was not the most elegant hotel in town, but it was conveniently close to the store. Of course, Max probably didn't care a rap about convenience, and he was no doubt on an expense account.

Oh, stop thinking about Max, she told herself irritably. Tomorrow morning will be plenty of time to deal with him. Why waste a pleasant evening on him, too?

She stood in the bedroom door and looked around. Yet another anonymous hotel room. Yet another room-service meal. Yet another unfamiliar bed, and a shower that took a mechanical engineer to operate, when all she had wanted tonight was her own small apartment and the peace and quiet her soul longed for. She sighed and started to strip off the uncrushable suit.

She took a long shower, wrapped her wet hair in a towel, and picked at a meal served on a tray at the small table in the living-room, with the television news as her only companion. After two weeks out of the country, she felt a little like a foreigner herself. She pushed her plate aside finally, and, too tired to care about drying her hair, slid between cool, anonymous white sheets.

If we're going to rent this suite for ever, she thought, we ought at least to decorate it to Tyler-Royale standards. It's embarrassing this way, with the industrial-grade green carpet and the plastic furniture . . .

But that was the last thought that slid through her weary mind. By eight o'clock that evening, central daylight time, Whitney Lattimer had slipped peacefully into sleep. She was too tired even to dream.

In any case, what happened some hours later was more nightmarish than dreamlike. She came awake abruptly as the bedroom lights glared, and sat up in the centre of the huge bed, blinking, scared to death.

The man with his hand on the light-switch seemed just as shocked as Whitney was, but he recovered sooner. 'Well,' he said, and though his voice was quiet it seemed

to fill the room with its vibrancy. 'Ross promised me all
the comforts of home if I'd take on this job, but I must
admit I didn't realise he was this good a friend!' His
eyes were roving appreciatively over her tumbled hair,
her almost-bare shoulders, her breasts under the delicate
lace gown.

Whitney abruptly realised that he was staring. She
pulled the sheet up to her chin. So this was Max
Townsend, she thought. Well, she couldn't say she was
surprised. He certainly was good looking, she decided,
if a woman liked the dark and arrogant self-assured type.
And that voice—yes, it would be possible to drown in
that voice. She pulled herself together.

'I assure you, Mr Townsend, that I was not sent to
Kansas City to be a—a playmate for you!'

'No? But you're supremely well qualified.' He started
towards the bed, slowly.

So this was Ross's precious consultant, she thought
resentfully. This was the man whose judgement Ross
trusted above all others! Wait till she told her brother
about this development; Max Townsend would look a
proper fool, then.

'No wonder the bellboy grinned and winked when I
said I didn't have any luggage,' he said thoughtfully.

This, Whitney decided, had gone far enough. She
shook her head, trying to clear her foggy brain. 'You
requested the presence of a Tyler-Royale executive,' she
reminded, 'so you could explain your findings. I am it.
So why don't you go back to wherever you've been
staying for the past two weeks, and I'll see you in the
morning. At the store. Goodnight, Mr Townsend.'

He didn't pause in his slow progress towards the bed,
and Whitney had to fight down a shiver. Hadn't the man
heard a word she said? For the first time she began to
realise that she was in a precarious position, and she
wondered if she could reach the bedside telephone in
time to call for help.

'But you see,' he said genially, 'it is already morning.'
He reached the windows and pulled the curtain back.
Full sunshine drenched the dark green carpeting. 'And
it's rather late morning at that.'

'Oh, no.' It was a mere breath. 'What time?'

'Nearly ten.'

She had slept straight through, for fourteen hours?
That's impossible, Whitney thought. It had still to be
the middle of the night. She wasn't ready for it to be
morning! But there was no arguing with the sunshine.
Max Townsend was right.

'This isn't usual for me,' she began, a little breathlessly.

Max Townsend merely lifted a disbelieving dark
eyebrow. He came back to the bed and sat down on the
edge of it, leaning against a pile of pillows. 'You certainly do a good imitation of it.'

If he wanted to be that way, she thought, let him! She
had tried to apologise.

'And your name?' he asked.

'Accept it as a challenge,' Whitney said acidly, sliding
away from him. 'I'll introduce myself at the store, in an
hour. In the meantime——'

Max took his jacket off, draped it across the foot of
the bed, and reached for the telephone. 'While you get
dressed, I'll order up some breakfast,' he said mildly.
'Bacon and eggs all right with you?'

Whitney's stomach lurched at the idea. 'If you're
hungry, why don't you go down to the restaurant?'

'Because then you would just go back to sleep. If you
can't get up in the morning, how do you manage to hold
down a job, Miss—?'

She ignored the question. She wasn't about to try ex-
plaining it to this arrogant snob. He probably thought
that jet-lag was all in the imagination!

But he obviously wasn't going to go away. How, she
wondered, could she get out of bed and to the chair where
her robe was lying with the least possible exposure? Then
she decided it didn't matter. What difference did it make

if Max Townsend got an eyeful? After all, she had been married. She would just pretend that it was Charles sitting there on the edge of the bed.

That thought was scarcely reassuring, she told herself crossly. She had to keep her wits about her. The last thing she needed was to start thinking about Charles. Dredging up memories of her brief and nightmarish marriage certainly wouldn't do her any good now.

A sudden shiver racked her at the thought of Charles. She tried to hide it and pushed the blankets back.

'Very nice,' Max murmured. 'No wonder Ross keeps you around.'

She glared at him and retreated to the bathroom. By the time she had showered and dressed, dragged a brush through her tangled black hair and put it into some semblance of order and applied her make-up, she felt a little better. She was at least prepared to meet Max Townsend again.

He was waiting for her in the living-room, reading the *Kansas City Times*. He glanced up as she emerged, ran an appraising eye over her pale blue suit, and turned back to the newspaper.

'Don't bother to stand up,' Whitney said acidly.

He smiled. 'Sorry. Most of the women I have breakfast with don't care about that sort of thing. They seem to feel that we've gone beyond formality by that time.'

Definitely the self-assured and arrogant type, she fumed.

'Have a cup of coffee,' he advised. 'It will probably make you feel a bit more human. I know it's difficult, being made to get up so early, but——'

'This is not early.'

'You can say that again. Breakfast?' He folded the newspaper and laid it aside.

She shuddered at the idea of food. 'Just coffee for me, thanks.'

'Oh, but I insist.' He piled scrambled eggs and bacon on a plate, added toast, and pushed it across the table towards her.

'I never eat breakfast.'

'You're probably never up early enough. What is your job at Tyler-Royale, anyway, Miss——?'

'The name is Lattimer. And don't worry about it; I assure you that I'm qualified to judge your report. Where is it, by the way?'

'Still in my head. I prefer to give my preliminary conclusions orally.'

'Well, I don't choose to receive them that way. Put everything in writing. I'll consider it and act as I see fit.'

'When you hear my conclusions, you may not want to have a written record, Miss Lattimer.'

'I can't imagine why not. And it's Mrs Lattimer.' The bacon did smell good, she had to admit. She picked up a crisp piece and broke it into bits.

Max Townsend leaned back in his chair, toying with his coffee spoon. His brown eyes had sharpened, and Whitney could almost see his brain clicking.

Then, abruptly, he relaxed. 'Now I have it,' he said comfortably. 'You're Ross's sister, the Merry Widow.'

'What difference that could possibly make to you is beyond my comprehension.'

'Oh, it matters a great deal,' he assured her. 'I was wondering if Ross had cracked, you see, to have put someone like you in top management. But the fact that you're his sister explains it all.'

It was perfectly bland, and it was the rankest insult Whitney had ever had to absorb. She bit her lip and then said, quietly, 'I'm glad to know that we agree on one thing at least—we share an opinion of each other. But since we do have to work together, Mr Townsend——'

'Make it Max. The staff would be suspicious at the formality, and we will need to have a united front if we're to work the miracles it will take to keep this store afloat.'

Whitney set her coffee-cup down with a bang. 'I don't know where you got the idea that you are going to revamp this store, Mr Townsend. Your job is to make your report, and then it is up to the management to decide what to do about it. We have a very effective manager here, and he is quite capable of taking any action that is necessary.'

Max wasn't looking at her. He was, with careful precision, reassembling the sections of the newspaper into their original order. Then he stood up. 'Thanks for breakfast, Mrs Lattimer,' he said cheerfully.

'What do you mean, thanks for breakfast?'

'Isn't it obvious? I charged it to your room account. I'll tell Ross what a——' He paused, and then went on with an ironic twist '—what a pleasure it was to meet you.'

'Where are you going?'

He stopped at the door. 'I should have thought it was obvious,' he pointed out. 'I'm going back to my office, where I'm going to call Ross and ask him to send someone down who wants to talk.'

'You haven't even given me your report yet.'

'Why waste my time? You've already decided to do nothing about it.'

Whitney shrugged. 'I admit that I can't take it too seriously. If your conclusions aren't important enough to write down——'

'I never said they weren't. I said that I wanted to show you the conditions first. Until you've seen them for yourself, the report will be useless. Once I've shown you what is going on down there, even you might decide I know what I'm talking about.' His voice was heavy with sarcasm.

'Just what conditions are you referring to?'

He stared at her for a moment, as if trying to make up his mind. 'Come on,' he said. 'I'll show you what I mean.'

This whole episode is a waste of time, Whitney told herself, and as soon as I can talk to Ross, I'll tell him that. But, since she was here, she supposed she might as well see what Max Townsend considered evidence. Then she could cut him to ribbons when she made her report to Ross. So she picked up her handbag and followed him.

'If these conditions you speak of are really there,' Whitney said, pulling the suite door shut behind her, 'I assume that you have told the store manager about them?'

'Apparently Ross didn't fill you in completely. I've been working undercover.'

'Behind the manager's back? Do you mean to tell me that Pete Ward doesn't even know you've been studying the store?'

'That's right. The fewer people who know, the less chance the news will slip out. Then I can see the store as it really is, and not when it's on its best behaviour.'

'A Tyler-Royale store is always at its best.'

Max gave her a pitying glance as he opened the door of a small black sports car, but didn't answer.

'Where did you get the financial information?' Whitney asked suddenly. 'Or don't you have any of that, yet?'

'From Ross, of course. He sent me the latest balance sheets.'

'I can't believe that he went behind Pete's back to plant a spy——'

'I am not a spy. And it wasn't Ross's idea. It was my condition for taking on the job.'

'Now that I can believe.' She maintained a haughty silence until they reached the bustling Country Club Plaza, the blocks-square shopping-area which had been the first planned development of its kind in the country. 'Pete Ward is one of our best managers,' she said. 'I cannot go along with him not knowing about this investigation.'

Max gave her a sideways glance. 'Are you always this inflexible?' he asked pleasantly. 'I suppose you're going to run right in and tell him that he's being used.'

Whitney frowned. She didn't like the way Max made it sound. 'Not exactly,' she said. 'But I will tell him why I'm here.'

'Well, before you do that,' Max said, pulling the sports car into a parking-spot across from the Tyler-Royale store, 'why don't you give me another few minutes of your precious time?'

'Doing what?' Whitney asked suspiciously.

'Nothing that you couldn't write home to Mother about, that's sure.' Max's voice was dry. 'How about a sporting proposition, Mrs Lattimer? Give me your full attention for ten minutes. If I can't convince you in that time that this store is dying, then you can go and talk to Pete Ward, and I'll call Ross and tell him that I've flipped.'

The words were jesting, but the tone wasn't. 'Dying?' Whitney said quietly. 'Do you really think the problem is that severe?'

'I'm not trying to keep you here because of your charm, that's sure.'

She ignored the sharpness of his tone. After all, she reminded herself, she was here for the good of Tyler-Royale, and she couldn't leave just because Max Townsend was an arrogant idiot. 'All right,' she said, 'you have ten minutes. Convince me.'

CHAPTER TWO

MAX looked at her for a moment as if he didn't believe what he had heard. Then he got out of the car and slammed the door.

'Where are you going?' Whitney called, scrambling out of the low seat.

'Come on.' He strode up the pavement with her trailing behind, stopped beside a recent model, cream-coloured car, and opened a rear door. 'Get in.'

'Shouldn't we go into the store?'

'That will come later.'

Whitney looked suspiciously at the car. 'What is this, a kidnapping?'

'Why on earth would I want you?'

'Thanks a lot.' She slid into the back seat of the car. A young woman behind the wheel gave her an abstracted smile and made a tally mark on a clipboard.

Max followed. 'Though I'm sure, come to think of it, that Ross would pay the ransom. I bet he'd come up with at least a dollar or two to get you back safely. Mrs Lattimer—Cindy Bell.'

The young woman in the front seat shifted the clipboard and reached over the seat to shake hands.

'What does it look like this morning, Cindy?' Max asked.

Cindy released the top sheet from the clipboard and handed it to him, without a word. She turned away again; she seemed to be watching the main entrance of the Tyler-Royale store across the street.

Max added up the tallies and said, with grim satisfaction, 'Thirty-two shoppers have come out of the main doors since opening time. One was carrying a Tyler-Royale bag. Two had big shopping-bags; they might or might not have bought something here and dropped it into the bag where Cindy couldn't see it. The other twenty-nine left empty-handed.'

It was an unpleasant statistic, but only a statistic, Whitney reminded herself. 'So?'

'That's a little worse than usual. We've been watching all the exits, and on the average day, one shopper out of twenty walks out with a bag or a box.'

Whitney shrugged. 'This survey is unscientific, to say the least.'

'Very true. But it's puzzling, and disquieting, that so few customers are actually buying at Tyler-Royale.'

'We have delivery services, you know——'

'So do some of the other department stores in the Plaza.' Max reached across the seat for a folder. 'Just to compare the figures, I've had a team watching them as well. Not one of them is as low as Tyler-Royale, and one consistently sends half its customers out with a purchase.'

'May I see those figures?' Whitney reached for the folder.

'My pleasure.'

'A big advertising campaign would skew these results terribly, you know,' she said pleasantly, looking down at the tally sheets. 'And the shopping crowds will vary dramatically from day to day.' But she couldn't deny that the figures were a shock. Why were so many of Tyler-Royale's customers going away empty-handed?

Max's dark eyes flared. 'I do know that much about my business, Mrs Lattimer,' he growled. 'The surveys were run on the same days, and we were careful to choose times when no sales or major ad campaigns were going on.'

The young woman in the front seat made no comment, but her eyebrows lifted as though she was startled. Whitney wondered why; if Cindy Bell had worked with Max for any time at all, surely she wasn't surprised to hear the irritable tone in his voice.

Whitney handed the folder back. 'So tell me why,' she challenged.

'That's what we asked ourselves.'

'We?'

'My staff and I,' Max said impatiently. 'You must remember that at this point, all we'd been doing was counting. None of us had yet been inside the store—officially, at least.'

'I can't see what the big secret was.'

'You will. For the last week, we've had shoppers going in and out. Sometimes they buy something, sometimes they appear to be just browsing. But they have a checklist of things to look for in a store. Again, they ran the same survey in the other stores as a comparison.'

'And?' Whitney prompted.

'Some departments were worse than others, but——'

The young woman in the front seat interrupted. 'I think she should see for herself, Max. I know I didn't believe it.'

'Believe what?' Whitney asked. 'You act as if there's a werewolf loose in ladies' lingerie.'

Max ignored the comment. He was looking her over thoughtfully. 'I think you have a point, Cindy,' he said. 'The lady is a little hard to convince. How well known are you in that store, Mrs Lattimer?'

Whitney shrugged. 'I haven't been there in six months,' she said. 'Since the Grand Opening. I know the manager, of course. He used to be in the Chicago store, as a department head. And I've met several of the buyers and supervisors——'

'Anybody in the electronics section?' Cindy asked crisply.

'I don't think so.'

'Then try electronics. Here.' The girl handed her a wide-brimmed straw hat. 'This will shade your face, just in case.'

Whitney took it reluctantly. 'It doesn't go very well with my suit.'

'All the better,' Cindy said calmly. She turned her attention back to the main doors.

'I'll go with you,' Max said.

'I don't even know what I'm doing!' She found herself on the pavement.

'That is probably the truest thing you've said all day,' he mused. 'I won't give you the whole checklist to do. All you have to do is walk into the department, browse, perhaps ask a question of a salesperson, and make a mental note of your feelings.'

'This is insane,' Whitney muttered.

Max smiled. 'Market research isn't as plush a job as you thought, is it, Mrs Lattimer?'

'It's Whitney,' she said reluctantly. If he called her 'Mrs Lattimer' once more, with that snide twist, she would hit him.

'I am honoured,' he said, and held the main door for her.

Electronics was on the far corner of the second level. Whitney had to pass Women's Sportswear to reach it, and she looked hurriedly around her, hoping that the buyer wouldn't happen on to the floor just then. Whitney had met her during their management-training days, and to run into the girl right now would be a disaster. But she reached the television, stereos and computers without seeing a familiar face, and she sighed in relief.

'What's your first reaction?' Max asked softly. 'Don't stop to think about it.'

'Clean,' Whitney said. 'Well stocked. Attractive.'

He murmured something that might have been either approval or disagreement.

'You want me to pick out something here and ask an intelligent question?'

Max swallowed a smile. 'It doesn't even have to be intelligent, Whitney.'

'Thanks a lot.' She moved a few feet away, and displayed fierce attention on a stereo system. Out of the corner of her eye, she saw two salesmen chatting, and she racked her brain. Quick, now, Whitney, she told herself. One of them is starting to come in this direction. Think of a question. What would a potential buyer want to know about this stereo?

The salesman walked by. 'Could you——' Whitney began.

He nodded. 'Good morning, ma'am,' he said briskly, and was gone before she could frame a word.

She stood in front of the stereo for another five minutes. The salesman returned, but this time he didn't even pause beside her. Instead, he disappeared into the stockroom.

Whitney moved to the counter and looked at cameras. Then she stood and tapped her fingers on the glass top for another few minutes. The second salesman was deeply absorbed in putting sales tags on calculators. He appeared to be blissfully unaware of her existence.

'Excuse me,' Whitney said, finally.

The clerk turned. 'Oh—I'll be right with you, ma'am.'

'I only wanted to ask——'

'I'll be there in just a moment, ma'am.' His voice was firm.

Whitney fell silent, but she was thoughtfully nibbling on a manicured nail by the time the man put his new merchandise carefully in a cabinet, arranging it just so. Then, with a cheerful smile, he came across to greet her. 'And what can I help you with this morning?'

Whitney smiled at him. It was quite a devastating smile; the salesman wasn't the first man to be nearly rocked off his feet by the sheer charm of it. But her voice contained only ice as she said. 'The only thing I want at the moment is to see the manager of this store. Immediately.'

The salesman faltered. 'But, ma'am——'

Max materialised beside her. His hand was firm on Whitney's elbow. 'I really don't think we have time this morning, darling,' he said smoothly. 'We'll come back another day.'

Whitney started to protest, and Max's fingers clenched on her arm.

She was at the front entrance before she regained her voice. 'What was the meaning of that?' she asked irritably, pulling away from Max and rubbing her wounded elbow. 'I could have shown Pete——'

'Just what could you have shown him? An insolent clerk in electronics? And how would you explain the fact that you were there at all?' He took her arm. 'Let's go and have lunch and talk it over.'

'You just ate breakfast,' Whitney grumbled. 'I only wanted to talk to Pete.'

'Do you really want to make a full explanation just now?'

'I wouldn't have to tell him everything.'

'Well, I don't think he would believe that you flew down here on a whim to buy a cordless phone, Whitney.'

'It was a camera,' she said. 'And by the way, if you ever call me darling again, I'll pick up the nearest heavy object and hit you with it.'

'Local colour,' Max said. 'I had to get you out of there somehow.'

Despite her protests against eating, she found herself a few moments later sitting at a marble-topped table in the ice-cream parlour next door to Tyler-Royale. 'I don't want anything to eat.'

Max ignored her and ordered two turkey club sandwiches.

'You're a bit of a dictator, aren't you?' There was no answer; Whitney had not expected one. She pulled off the hat with relief and tossed it on to a chair. 'Why did you drag me out of there?' she asked baldly. 'Why didn't you want me to protest to Pete?'

'Because I didn't want you firing off a cannon where a rifle would do. Or taking a potshot at some poor clerk if the problem really requires the heavy artillery. The trouble is, at the moment we don't know which it will take.'

'What do you mean, some poor clerk? That problem should have been taken care of immediately,' Whitney said stubbornly.

'Yes—if it was an isolated case. But the fact is, Whitney, that every one of my employees who goes into Tyler-Royale has reported the same sort of thing. Usually they're not ignored, but they've been talked down to, or talked about behind their backs. There is a disease in that store. And worse, it couldn't have got that bad unless top management condoned it.'

The sandwiches arrived, and Whitney absently took a bite. 'You can't make me believe that Pete approves of that sort of thing. It's his store that is at stake.'

'I didn't say he approves of it. But he apparently isn't doing anything to stop it.'

'Perhaps he doesn't know about it.'

'Perhaps. But if not—why doesn't he? If it was obvious to you in less than fifteen minutes, how could he avoid knowing?'

'Good question,' she said reluctantly.

'It's something like pruning a blighted tree,' Max went on. 'There is no sense in lopping off twigs if the main trunk is diseased.'

Whitney sighed. 'All right. You're the expert. Where do we cut?'

There was a brief silence, and then Max said, 'I thought I was only supposed to make a report, which management would act on.'

Whitney looked up in shock, to meet a quiet twinkle in his dark eyes. She propped her elbows on the edge of the table and smiled at him, just as she had at the salesman. But where the salesman had stammered, Max merely lifted an eyebrow. 'You're right,' she said confidingly. 'I've treated you abominably all morning, and I deserved that. So let's bury the sword——'

'And pound the hatchet into a ploughshare?'

'Something like that. How about it, partner?'

He didn't speak right away, and when he did, it wasn't an answer at all. 'You're as complicated as a headache, Whitney Lattimer,' he murmured. 'And something tells me you could be just as hard to figure out. Eat your sandwich.'

She did, obediently. 'What do we do next?' she asked.

'First, we bring you up to date. Then we begin doing exit polls—start talking to every shopper coming out, whether she bought anything or not.'

'Can you do that, without Pete's knowledge?'

'Sure.' He grinned, suddenly. 'I have you, don't I? What else could a man need?'

By six o'clock Whitney had learned more about unorthodox methods of marketing research than she had ever imagined there was to know. She had talked to several of Max's professional shoppers—most of them women—and had learned that well dressed and prosperous-looking customers usually received better treatment than others at Tyler-Royale. 'It's an attitude thing,' Cindy Bell had tried to explain. 'It's as if the salespeople don't want to talk to anyone who hasn't got big money.'

'Two of them ignored me,' Whitney mused. 'I can't say that I look my best today, but——'

'It might have been the hat,' Cindy giggled.

'Oh, dear!' Whitney was horrified to be reminded of the hat. 'I must have left it in the ice-cream shop.'

'That's all right. I never did like it, really, but it was useful for this kind of work.'

'I'll buy you any one you want at the store, to replace it.'

Cindy grinned. 'I think I'll wait till you take over. Then I know there'll be a salesclerk around!'

Whitney smiled and agreed. Everyone on Max's payroll seemed convinced that she had been sent to Kansas City as the store's new manager. She didn't enlighten them. If Peter Ward wasn't able to continue in his position, then Ross would transfer someone else. In the meantime, her job was troubleshooter; why cause herself any additional problems?

But she mentioned it to Max when he took her back to the hotel. 'Perhaps I should have told Cindy I won't be staying,' she said.

'Why bother? She'll be involved in another project by then, and it won't make any difference to her.'

'That's true, but I owe her a hat regardless. Thanks for the ride, Max.'

'I'll walk you up.'

Whitney raised an eyebrow. 'I'm a big girl,' she pointed out. 'I can make my way through dangerous hotel halls alone.'

'The least I can do to restore my gentlemanly image is to carry this load of statistics up.'

'Oh.' Whitney looked at the stack of papers in the back seat and sighed. It would take hours to digest all that information, and she would have to do it before the investigation could go much further. 'I'd forgotten those. In that case, be my guest.'

As they walked down the hall to Whitney's suite, she added, 'You must enjoy your job.'

'I do. But what brought you to that conclusion?'

She smiled. 'I don't know. Being surrounded by women of every age and description seems like the sort of thing you would enjoy.'

'Every second of it.'

They turned the last corner, and Whitney's steps faltered. 'Oh, no.'

'What?'

'It's Pete Ward,' she muttered. 'I had no idea I was supposed to stay hidden, Max, or I wouldn't have used the suite at all.'

The man standing at the suite door turned at the sound of voices. 'Whitney!' he said, coming toward her. 'I didn't know you were even in town till just an hour ago. What's the surprise?'

'Oh—hello, Pete,' she said weakly. 'It—well, this trip came up rather suddenly, and there just wasn't time to let you know.' Should I introduce Max, and give the whole thing away, she wondered frantically, or look rude by ignoring the fact that he's standing here? Would Pete even recognise Max's name?

Beside her, Max extended a hand. 'Nice of you to stop by to welcome us,' he said. 'Would you care for a drink?' He pulled a key from his pocket and unlocked the suite door, very much the host at ease with an unexpected guest. He ushered Whitney in, with a possessive hand on the small of her back.

Pete Ward's eyes almost popped from his head. 'Oh—no, thanks. I just stopped to see if you'd like to have dinner with me, Whitney. I guess not, though, hmm?' He was sizing up Max with sidelong, darting glances.

Whitney groaned inwardly. Then she said, with a brittle catch in her voice, 'Thanks, Pete. But I've made plans for the evening.'

'Sure. I—I sure didn't mean to interrupt anything.' The manager beat a hasty retreat down the hall.

'Sorry about that,' Max said, pushing the door wide. 'It seemed to me we had a choice——'

Whitney turned on him irritably. 'So you sacrificed my reputation instead of the project. You do realise that he thinks we're shacked up here together?'

'Of course. What else could any reasonable person think?'

Whitney groaned. Then, with an effort, she swallowed her indignation. Max had only done what was necessary, after all. 'I suppose you got that key at the desk this morning.'

'That's right,' he agreed cheerfully. 'How did you think I got in?'

She hadn't considered the question; she hadn't had time to wonder. She decided, now, that she would rather not know what the desk clerk had been told. 'Would you at least turn the key back in, please?' she asked.

'Sure. Anything you want.' He put the stack of folders on the small dining-table. 'Well,' he said, rubbing the back of his hand along his jaw, 'I guess I'll be going. You'll be all right here?'

She looked up in shocked disbelief. 'I've been in much more dangerous places than Kansas City, all by myself.'

'Of course.'

She followed him to the door, wondering what was bothering him. He seemed uneasy, uncomfortable. It didn't seem to fit with the assured Max she had watched all day. Then a possible cause occurred to her. 'Max——'

He turned.

'Where are you staying?'

His smile flashed. 'Why? In case you want me in the middle of the night?'

'Don't kid yourself.'

'Or are you concerned that I might be inconvenienced because I'm being a gentleman and leaving the suite to you?'

'It did cross my mind,' Whitney said tartly. 'Of course, I immediately dismissed the notion that you were a gentleman. But with the convention in town, there aren't any hotel rooms available.'

'The city is full of people,' he agreed.

'Where have you and your harem been staying?'

'Is this an invitation to stay here?' His eyes were bright.

'Not at all,' Whitney snapped.

Max relented. 'Don't you and Ross ever communicate?' he asked curiously. 'I live in Kansas City—just about two miles south of the Plaza, as a matter of fact.'

'Oh.' She felt like an idiot.

'I travel some, of course, especially when I'm working for Ross. But most of my business is right here in Kansas City.'

'Well, I'm glad you're not out in the cold.' She sounded a little tart.

Max just grinned. 'Even consultants have to live somewhere. Surprising, isn't it? I'll bet you thought I folded up at night and disappeared into the brickwork.'

'I assumed you retreated into a cave somewhere and did the paperwork.' She gestured toward the table. 'How do you keep up with it all? I'll be hours wading through that.'

'You're the one who insisted on reading every word.' He didn't sound sympathetic.

'Aren't there any short cuts?' It had been a long day, and studying raw tally sheets and preliminary reports was the least exciting thing she could think of, on top of jet-lag.

Max looked her over, head to toes, and said, soberly, 'Only if you trust me to interpret the results accurately.'

She sighed. 'All right. I surrender. Will you boil it down for me?'

He didn't answer. 'You told Pete Ward you had plans for the evening.'

'I do,' she said with a smile. 'Room service usually has decent chicken. Sometimes it's even still warm by the time it's delivered.'

'Why don't you have dinner with me?' Max said abruptly. 'We can talk about the survey in comfort.'

She was horrified. She knew that she must have sounded plaintive, but she hadn't expected this. 'Look, I wasn't trying to cadge an invitation,' she began.

'I know. It's quite apparent that you haven't much use for me. But it's only business—surely you can put up with me for a couple more hours?'

She didn't answer right away. What graceful way was there to get out of this? She had practically forced the man to issue the invitation.

'Besides,' Max added, with a twinkle in his dark eyes, 'no matter where you have dinner, Ross will end up paying for it. So why waste an evening on room service?'

She had to laugh at that. 'If you're sure,' she said. 'But I'd like to change first.'

'And you'd like me to leave while you do it.'

'My goodness, perhaps you're a gentleman after all!'

'I do have occasional flashbacks of my mother's teaching.' He glanced at his watch. 'I'll meet you in the lobby in an hour.'

'How long do you think I need to make myself beautiful?'

Max grinned. 'I'll be waiting,' he promised.

Whitney stood staring at the door for a full minute after he left. Now why, she wondered, did I let myself in for a whole evening with Max Townsend?

To avoid the paperwork, she reminded herself. She yawned and retreated to the bedroom to search through her luggage for an outfit that was still fit to wear. Two weeks on the other side of the Pacific had nearly exhausted her wardrobe. 'I knew I should have sent everything to the cleaners before I came home,' she said, with a yawn.

She was in the shower when the phone rang, and she grabbed a short terry robe and hurried out to answer it.

'I'm glad you're back in communication,' Ross said. His voice was light, but there was a repressed note of excitement, too.

Whitney pulled off her wet shower-cap, piled the pillows up, and leaned against them. 'What's up, Ross?'

'You have a seven-pound nephew, born this afternoon. Andrew Patrick Clayton.'

Whitney silently thanked heaven that she was the one in Kansas City, and not Ross. 'I'll bet Kelly's glad it's over,' she said.

'She's tired out, but she's fine. Whit, the baby is so wrinkled and red and ugly——'

She laughed. 'You don't sound disappointed.'

'And he's perfect. He even has all his fingers and toes.'

'You expected this baby to be born with fins? Look, Ross, I hate to bring you back to earth, but it looks as if I may be here for a while, and my travelling wardrobe is reaching the end. Could you send me some clothes? Air express, please.'

'Buy whatever you want.' He sounded as clothes were the last thing anyone should be concerned about.

'I don't need any more. I have cupboards full at home. It's just that I need them here instead of in Chicago.

'Charge them to me. What do you think of Max?'

She frowned just a little. 'He's on to something, Ross.'

'I told you he knew what he was talking about. Watch out for him, though. He's a bit of a ladies' man.'

'I had managed to figure that out,' Whitney said drily. 'In any case, don't worry about me. I'm immune to men—especially ones who have an eye for the ladies.'

There was a brief silence. 'I didn't mean that he was anything like Charles.'

'I'm convinced that every man, given the opportunity, is something like Charles. All but you, of course.' She curled up against the pillows.

'He really was a bastard, wasn't he?'

'Must we talk about Charles? The man has been dead for three years.'

'He might be buried,' Ross said, 'but he isn't dead at all. Not as long as you compare every man out there to him.'

'Please stop, Ross——'

'All right. I know I'm treading on sacred ground. Any report to make on the store?'

'Not yet. I'll call you in a day or two, when I know a little more. Give my love to Kelly and the baby.'

Reminded of his new son, Ross went into raptures again. 'Andrew is really a terrific baby, Whit,' he confided. 'He's got a lot of black hair and dark blue eyes——'

'Yes, Dad,' she teased. 'Now let me get back to work so I can finish this job and come home to admire the paragon!'

She put the phone down and leaned back against the pillows for a moment, her eyes closed. Why had she agreed to have dinner with Max? she wondered. She wouldn't be able to stay awake. And why, having done so, hadn't she told Ross?

It was no big deal, she reminded herself. Why would Ross care? He wasn't her keeper, after all...

A warm hand came to rest on her shoulder. 'Charles?' she murmured, sleepily, and then pulled away as if she had been burned. 'Don't touch me,' she said.

'Whitney? Wake up.'

That wasn't Charles's voice. It was more like the rich notes of a pipe-organ. She struggled up from the depths, and tried to focus her eyes. 'Max?' she said thickly. 'You said you'd wait in the lobby.'

'I waited. And waited. And waited. Finally I came back to see if you'd stood me up. Have you contracted the sleeping-sickness bug, or what? You were so sound asleep when I came in that I thought for a minute you were dead.'

She sat up, and only realised when she met his eyes just how little the terry robe left to the imagination. 'I'll be ready in a minute,' she said, with dignity, and marched across to the bathroom, her head high.

'I've heard that one before,' he teased.

'You could wait in the living-room,' she pointed out.

'Not me,' he said. 'I've learned my lesson. No more being a gentleman around you, Whitney. A man could starve to death that way.'

Whitney slammed the bathroom door, but it didn't quite close out the sound of his laugh.

CHAPTER THREE

From the restaurant, perched high atop a tower, Kansas City was a grid of gold and yellow lights spreading as far as Whitney could see. To the north was the downtown area, where unfinished skyscrapers bulked dark against lighted towers beyond, hints of the skyline of the future, after the city's massive construction campaign was done.

'What would you say,' Whitney asked curiously, turning back to Max, 'if I told you right now that revolving restaurants make me seasick?'

'I'd offer to eat your dinner as well as my own,' he said promptly.

'You don't look like a glutton.' As far as she could see, there wasn't an excess ounce of flesh anywhere on him.

'I worry it all off.'

He has an answer for everything, she thought idly. I'd feel much less threatened by Max Townsend if he would show just a hint of bad taste here and there. A garish necktie, perhaps.

She looked thoughtfully across the table. His neatly striped silk tie gave her no opening. She wondered if he had bought it at the hotel gift shop just for the occasion; he certainly hadn't been wearing a tie earlier. His navy blazer and grey trousers were casual but well tailored.

And she couldn't fault his taste in restaurants either. The service was superb, and the wine she was sipping was just dry enough, just cold enough, without excess.

Silly, she thought. Would you really have preferred the wine to be warm and sour, just so that you could turn up your nose at his taste? Why not just enjoy it while it lasts?

She didn't paused to wonder why she was feeling threatened by Max Townsend.

The silence was comfortable, and she sighed. 'I suppose we should get down to business,' she said reluctantly.

'Must we? Let's have dinner first.'

'You said you'd help me with——'

'So I got you here under false pretences,' he interrupted. 'Would you really rather be eating cold chicken in your room?'

Whitney looked out over the golden lights. 'No. Of course not.' She smiled across at him. 'Thank you for suggesting this, Max.'

'Good. There's one for my side.' He swirled the wine in his glass. 'Do you travel a lot?'

'Too much for my taste, sometimes. I'm on the road about half the time, and I get tired of hotel rooms.'

He nodded. 'The glamour wears off, doesn't it? That's why I restrict myself to Kansas City now, unless it's a project I really want to do.'

'Unfortunately, someone at Tyler-Royale has to do the travelling.'

'I thought Ross liked running around the country like a kangaroo, checking up on all the stores.'

'He used to. But since he got married, his idea of happily-ever-after includes staying at home. And now, with the baby, it will be even harder to get him out of Chicago.'

Max nodded thoughtfully. She had told him Ross's big news on the way to the restaurant.

'So I've been doing it instead,' Whitney said.

'There's nothing keeping you at home? You and what's-his-name didn't have kids?'

'Charles,' she supplied, absently, without even wondering why he had bothered to ask. Once, she remembered, she had wanted a child. Once she had thought that might make a difference.

'Oh, yes. I remember.'

'Remember?' she asked, puzzled. 'What do you mean?'

'You said his name tonight when I woke you.'

'Did I?'

There was a long silence. Then Max said, softly, 'You must miss him very much.'

What else did I say, she wondered, with a touch of panic. 'Why do you ask?'

He stared into his wine-glass, and then looked up. 'You were hugging your pillow when I walked in, as if you were pretending that it was him.'

Whitney hoped that she wasn't changing colour. 'I see,' she said coolly. 'To answer your question—no, Charles and I never had a child. We'd been married less than two years when——' she hesitated for a second, and then firmly, '—when he died.'

He nodded. 'Of course, it's none of my business,' he said.

'That's correct.' There was a tinge of ice in her voice.

Why don't you just drop it, Max? she thought. Please don't cross-examine me about Charles. Ross was right: the man is dead and should be forgotten.

'You're thinking that I'm being nosy,' Max said.

She met his eyes. There was warm good humour in his gaze. 'Yes, I was,' she admitted. 'But I shouldn't have been surprised. Gossip is a way of life for you, isn't it?'

'Not gossip,' he corrected quickly. 'A gossip spreads rumour. I gather facts. Actually, I'm a professional busybody.'

She had to laugh at that. 'Did Ross assign you to check up on me, too?'

'Oh, no. This is strictly a personal interest.'

An icy shiver of warning trickled down her spine. She didn't want him to take a personal interest in her. She was done with all that. Since Charles had died, she had kept her distance from all men—all but Ross. Max Townsend wasn't going to change that.

'I don't understand the attraction of marriage,' Max went on. 'Look at what it does to people. As a matter of fact, I'm still reeling from the shock of Ross taking the plunge.'

'You didn't expect it?' She felt a little silly, but relieved. It had been a bit stupid of her to jump to the conclusion that he had felt some kind of romantic attraction to her! Max was merely indulging a bit of idle curiosity.

'Of course not. How could he do this to me? We were going to treasure our freedom forever and love the ladies with just enough detachment to keep us safe from any entanglements. And then he has to spoil it all, and leave me as the last defence of bachelordom.'

Whitney smiled in spite of herself at the mournful tone of his voice. 'I'm sure you'll be able to hold up the standards quite well by yourself,' she said soothingly. 'You seem to get plenty of practice in your work, at least.'

Max looked wounded. 'You aren't taking me seriously,' he accused.

'Of course I am. And you shouldn't be upset at the idea of being the sole representative of the breed, Max. You make such a perfect example.'

'Are you laughing at me?'

'I wouldn't dream of it.' But she was maintaining a straight face with an effort.

Max shook his head. 'Whenever I imagine Ross sitting by the fire surrounded by kids, I get nervous.'

'He's not exactly surrounded,' Whitney said. 'Andrew is only one very small baby.'

'There'll be more,' Max predicted direly. 'There always are. I just don't comprehend how any man can tie himself down so much.'

'And Ross does such a good job of pretending to be happy about it, too.' Then Whitney sobered, suddenly. 'You're actually serious, aren't you, Max?'

'Of course I am. I simply don't understand this passion for making things legal. With divorce becoming the national pastime, why take the chance?'

'Because people still believe in marriage. They think it's possible to live happily ever after.' Her voice held a tinge of sadness.

'You're living proof of that, you know.'

'Me?' She was startled. 'I don't believe in fairy tales any more, if that's what you mean.'

'No. But your husband is dead, and you've thrown yourself into your work. The sensible thing to do would have been to look around for someone else to enjoy yourself with. But the fact that you'd been married kept you faithful to his memory—to the fairy-tale ending.'

For one awful, angry moment, Whitney contemplated tipping her glass of wine over his head and walking out of the restaurant. Had Ross been talking about her to Max? The idea made her even more furious.

And no matter where Max's information might have come from, how dared this arrogant fool tell her what was wrong with her life? What business of his was it? How could Max, who by his own admission had never been serious about a woman, possibly know what forces had made Whitney as she was?

He didn't have his facts straight, that was certain. She realised with a breath of relief that his knowledge couldn't have come from Ross. If it had, he wouldn't have made these assumptions—he would have known the truth. For Ross, of course, knew everything there was to know. It was a little comfort to know that at least her brother hadn't given her away.

Ross had understood, as no other man ever could. And there was no reason why she should even attempt to explain herself to anyone else, especially this professional busybody, as he had so correctly described himself. But Max Townsend wouldn't be easy to shut up, she knew.

She took a deep breath. 'What makes you so certain of that?' she asked pleasantly. 'What would you like to know about my private life, Max?'

'Lots of things,' he said promptly. 'I just like knowing what makes people tick.'

'What if I were to tell you that I've decided not to allow myself to fall in love again? Would that surprise you? Perhaps I've decided to have a man in every town, and to love him and leave him at my convenience. You men do that sort of thing—why shouldn't a woman have satisfying physical affairs without emotional involvement?'

Max smiled. 'How very interesting,' he said, reaching for her hand across the table and raising it till her fingers cupped his jaw. 'We may have something in common after all, Whitney. Because, you see, since I walked into your bedroom this morning, I've wanted to make love to you.'

For an instant, Whitney thought her teasing threat of being seasick on the revolving restaurant was going to come true. It felt to her as if the mechanism that guided the slow-moving circle on its endless rounds had suddenly gone haywire, jerking and swaying and going a hundred miles an hour. She snatched her fingers from Max's grip, and said, tightly, 'I don't find that humorous. Or flattering.'

Max laughed. 'I didn't think you would. Take my advice, Whitney. Stay out of poker games—you're lousy at bluffs.'

Whitney stared at the base of her wine glass.

'I'm sorry,' he said. 'I should have realised long before this that Charles is a delicate subject—one you do not wish to discuss. I'm not usually quite so clumsy about that sort of thing, but I wanted to know, you see, and so I plunged right on.'

'I don't see why you had to pry into my private concerns.' She knew she sounded sullen, and she didn't care.

'Don't you?'

She looked up, then, and was startled by the brilliant brown blaze of his eyes. But before she could ask a question, or even know what it was she wanted to ask, he smiled at her and began to talk easily of books, and music, and plays they both had seen. Within a few minutes Whitney had relaxed.

Max wasn't such a bad guy after all, she thought. A little too curious about things that didn't concern him, of course. But, on the whole, not bad. No wonder Ross liked him so.

They drove through Country Club Plaza after dinner. The stores and shops were closed, of course, but the Plaza itself was never really deserted. The restaurants and nightspots and theatres were still open, and on every street there were couples walking hand in hand, and groups of teenagers out for the evening, despite the autumn chill in the air. But even in the dead of winter the Plaza would never be empty.

Max parked the little sports car in front of Tyler-Royale, and they joined the parade of strollers. Max casually took her hand, and Whitney just as unconcernedly drew it away. She was darned if she'd walk through the Plaza holding hands with Max Townsend!

'I don't understand,' Whitney murmured, looking up at the mass of subtly lighted brick and tile. 'This store has our best people, our best merchandise. How can it be in trouble?' Her eyes rested on the mannequin in the store window, wearing the latest imported fashion.

Max sighed. 'I don't know,' he said. 'But I feel responsible. I'm the one who picked the location.'

'Look around you. There is plenty of foot traffic, even at this hour. The location can't be the problem.'

'I've got it!' Max exclaimed, snapping his fingers. 'If the store would open at ten in the evening and stay open all night, it would please all these frustrated shoppers. And there would be no competition from the other stores.'

'Somehow, I don't think that's the answer, Max.' She noticed, idly, that her hand was now resting in the crook of his elbow; she had no idea how it had got there. She tried to pull unobtrusively away, but Max's arm was like a steel band holding her fast.

'Well, let's leave the store's problems till morning,' he said cheerfully. 'How about a carriage ride?'

The vehicles were lined up at the kerb, each pulled by a single horse and guided by a driver in formal coat and top-hat. Each carriage was different, some high-backed, some low-slung. One was white, with blue velvet upholstery. The rest were more soberly designed.

It looked like fun, Whitney thought, but would it be smart to encourage Max any further? No, she decided. Better to stay out of romantic carriages.

She shook her head. 'It's too chilly.' The autumn air was crisper than she had planned for, and the jacket of her linen suit was unlined. It made a perfect excuse, she thought.

'I'll keep you warm.'

That's what I'm afraid of, Whitney thought. But before she could gather her objections, Max was urging her towards the first carriage. Whitney gave in. What could she say, after all, that wouldn't create a scene?

'You aren't afraid of horses, are you?' he asked, handing her up.

'Of course not.' She settled herself carefully. The driver clucked to his horse and they were off.

'Technically, I suppose it's more of a buggy,' Whitney said, determined to keep the conversation on a casual level.

'But that sounds much less aristocratic than a carriage does.' His arm lay on the back of the seat, around her shoulders. 'Lean against me if you're cold.'

She sat very straight, determined not to encourage him. 'The Plaza looks different this way. Seeing it from a carriage, I mean.'

'I didn't think that you meant having my arm around you.' Before she could retort, he went on, 'Wait till you see it at Christmas time, with the lights lining every tree and building.'

The carriage took a corner fast and threw her against Max. His arm tightened to keep her close against him. 'We have a very considerate driver,' he murmured.

'That's one point of view,' Whitney said tartly. But she had to admit that he was right. The open carriage was warmer this way. She shifted her position slightly and let herself relax. It wasn't dignified to fight him, after all. Besides, pitting her strength against Max was obviously a losing battle.

It was pleasant, riding along the Plaza with the cool breeze in her face, with the rhythmic clop of hooves making a pattern in her ears, and with the gentle sway of the carriage rocking her into peaceful comfort, with Max's arm around her.

He smiled down at her, and for the first time Whitney realised what it was that women saw in Max Townsend. It wasn't just his good looks, dark and arrogant and compelling. It wasn't the lean build, or even the charming smile. It was the humour that lurked in his eyes and in the laugh-lines in his face. It was the gentle touch of his fingers against her cheek, and the tenderness in his first fleeting kiss.

For a few brief moments Whitney Lattimer forgot that she had long since decided never again to become involved with a man. She forgot that she didn't particularly like this man, and that they had spent much of the evening in a verbal fencing-match. And she even forgot that she was being chauffeured through Country Club Plaza in a an open, horse-drawn carriage, for all the world to see.

Sanity returned with a breathless crunch. One charming scoundrel is just like another, she thought. Gentleness and tenderness are a standard part of the scoundrel's bag of tricks.

Before she allowed herself to consider the possible consequences, the palm of her hand cracked against the side of Max's face.

He drew back, startled. Whitney huddled into the corner of the carriage, her eyes closed, trying to hide. Automatically, she had assumed a defensive posture, with her arms up, protecting her face.

'I don't hit women,' he said, his voice crackling with irritation. 'I never have, and despite the temptation you offer me, I don't intend to start now. So for heaven's sake sit up.'

Whitney opened her eyes, cautiously. There was a red mark on his cheek, and he was rubbing it and watching her warily.

'I'm sorry,' she said tentatively.

'No, I think that's my line.' The carriage drew to a halt, and Max said, 'May I help you out? Or am I taking my life in my hands if I touch you again?'

Whitney bit her lip, hard, till tears came to her eyes, and shook her head. Max lifted her down from the carriage, and she fumbled in her bag for a handkerchief. She wouldn't meet his eyes.

He drove her back to the hotel without a word. At the main entrance, Whitney turned toward him and said, 'Max, I'm sorry——'

'You shouldn't say you're sorry unless you really are,' he recommended. 'And it was apparent to me that you meant it when you slapped me. The communication was quite clear.'

'Will I see you tomorrow?' She could have kicked herself for asking. The tone of her voice was that of an uncertain child.

'I don't know. I do have other clients; has that ever occurred to you? Cindy will be in front of the store at opening-time. Look, Whitney, I have to move. The car is blocking the drive.'

There was obviously nothing else he wanted to say to her. And that's just fine, she told herself. I've nothing to say to him either.

She paused, though, with one foot on the cobbled drive. 'Thank you for dinner,' she said.

'I told you to thank Ross. It'll be on my expense account.' He didn't look at her.

'Goodnight, Max.'

There was a brief silence. Then he said, quietly, 'Goodnight, Sleeping Beauty.'

There was a twist in his voice that sounded almost angry. She puzzled over it until she got to her room. Then she dismissed it from her mind and almost fell into bed. The oblivion of sleep would be especially welcome tonight, she thought.

But despite her exhaustion, sleep didn't come. When she closed her eyes, all she could see was Max's face, startled and angry, in the instant after she had slapped him.

Yes, one charming scoundrel is just like another, she assured herself. There was no reason for her to feel guilty about what she had done. He had deserved to be set back on his heels.

Max's face blurred in her mind, and suddenly Charles was watching her from the darkness. He had looked at her like that once, she thought fuzzily. She couldn't remember what he had said, the precise words that had prompted her to slap him. But after she had, Charles had looked at her like that. She remembered the look, and she remembered getting up off the floor a moment later. She didn't recall the blow that had put her there.

And that had been the beginning. Only the beginning.

Max had been angry tonight, too, she thought. Remember it well, Whitney. One charming scoundrel is just like another...

And with that refrain running through her head, Whitney sighed and slept.

*   *   *

The wake-up call found her already alert, staring at the
ceiling and trying to be grateful that she was back on
normal time. But Max kept intruding, taking over her
thoughts. She owed him an apology, that was sure,
Whitney decided. All the man had done was to steal a
kiss; the proper response would have been to tell him
politely she wanted to keep their relationship on a businesslike basis. Max wasn't dense, and she wouldn't have
had to hit him to get the message across.

But she might not have the chance to tell him she was
sorry. He might not even show up today, she suspected.
He had other clients, after all, and the majority of his
work for Tyler-Royale was done. From now on, his staff
could conduct the interviews. All that would be required
of Max was to read and interpret the results, and he could
do that with a written report—the kind that had seemed
so important to her yesterday.

Yesterday, she thought. Was it only yesterday morning
that he had walked into the suite and almost dragged
her out of bed?

'You're being incredibly silly,' she told herself firmly,
'if you think that it could possibly matter whether or
not you apologise to Max Townsend. He's a professional; the work will get done. And you might actually
have done women in general a good turn last night, by
taking his impudence down a notch.'

But she wasn't convinced. If he didn't turn up today,
she decided, she would ask Cindy Bell for his address
and write him an apologetic note. Then she might feel
better. He might be a scoundrel or he might not, but
even if he was, it didn't excuse her behaviour.

She pushed back the blankets. Somehow, a little of
the excitement had gone out of the day. Straightening
out that store was beginning to look like a job and a
half, and she wasn't quite sure where to begin.

She was putting the last few hairpins in the smooth
twist of almost black hair when there was a quiet tap on
the main door of the suite.

'That's probably Pete Ward,' she murmured, 'trying to catch me in bed with my lover so he can report me to Ross.' She realised, abruptly, that her opinion of the manager had changed quite a bit since yesterday, and she was pondering that idea as she opened the door.

Max put a large foot firmly in the opening and held out two long-stemmed pink roses, one in each hand.

She took them carefully. 'What are these for?'

'I figured if you had both hands occupied with thorns, I'd at least have fair warning of an attack.'

She smiled wanly. 'I'm sorry, Max. I'm not just saying that, either. I really am sorry.'

'May I come in?'

She glanced down at his foot. 'It would be futile to refuse, wouldn't it?'

'Well, yes.'

'In that case, come in. What are you doing here?' She poked through the cabinet in the kitchenette, and came up with an iced-tea glass. The roses would look odd in it, but at least they would have water, she decided.

'I came to bring a peace offering.'

He didn't look very peaceable, she decided. He looked rather like a thundercloud instead, as he paced the living-room.

'Dammit, Whitney, why didn't you tell me?' he burst out.

'Tell you what?'

'I talked to Ross for a couple of hours last night,' he began.

Cold dread inched over Whitney, and her skin crawled. 'What did Ross tell you?' she whispered. He promised me, she was screaming inside. He promised me he would never tell anyone the horrible things I shared with him! He has no right to spread out my life to soothe Max's damaged ego——

Max leaned against the sink beside her, his palms braced on the counter-top. He looked furious. 'Why didn't you tell me you'd been awake for two days getting here? If I'd had any idea you were suffering from jet-lag, I wouldn't have treated you so badly. It's no wonder you slapped me last night. I deserved it for acting like a jerk when you were asleep on your feet.'

'Jet-lag?' Whitney whispered. 'Ross told you I came straight here from Tokyo?'

'It's a good thing he did tell me. You obviously never would have, Whitney.'

'I didn't think about it, it didn't seem important.' Then Ross hadn't said anything about Charles after all. Her taut nerves began to relax a little.

'No, and I wasn't thinking very well either. I laughed at you for falling asleep. I could kick myself for being so insensitive.'

'Well, don't. It isn't the end of the world.' She balanced the roses carefully in the glass and tried not to let herself feel so ridiculously glad that he was there.

'Whitney——' He sounded hesitant, like a shy little boy. 'Was it anything personal last night? When you slapped me, I mean.'

She was glad she was looking at the roses. He had given her the perfect opportunity. Now she would say something pleasant and comforting and businesslike, and then she would look up with a cool smile, and all would be well again. She would never be bothered with any more unwanted attentions, and they could work to-gether for as long as necessary.

She set the glass carefully on the coffee-table, smoothed her hair, and picked up her handbag. 'Of course it wasn't personal,' she said as she opened the door of the suite.

Max grinned. It was a sunny smile, as if she had re-stored his faith in the goodness of the universe. Then he reached for her hand. 'I didn't think it could be per-sonal,' he said cheerfully. 'If you'd taken a dislike to me, you wouldn't have kissed me like that.'

Whitney stopped dead in the middle of the hallway. 'What on earth do you mean, I kissed you?'

'You did, as a matter of fact, you know,' he confided. 'You really seemed to be enjoying yourself. That's why it took me so much by surprise when you belted me two seconds later.'

'I beg your pardon, but I most certainly did not——'

He kissed her fingertips, locked her hand in his, and started down the hall towards the lift, pulling her along. 'I'm so glad that you don't find me repellent,' he added gently. 'Because, you see, Whitney, I wasn't joking last night. I have a very lively desire to make love to you— and sooner or later, I intend to do it. Any objections?'

CHAPTER FOUR

SO MUCH for the idea of Max being a shy little boy,
Whitney thought in irritation as they drove across Kansas
City. For the fourth time in ten minutes, she said, 'I do
not want to have an affair with you, Max. This is a
business deal, and I want to keep it on a businesslike
basis.'

'I understand, Whitney.'

'You do?' She felt a bit of shock; he certainly hadn't
seemed to hear her the first three times she had said it.

'Of course. A lady always protests before giving in.'

'This is not a mere idle protest, dammit!'

'But we both understand what you really want.'

'What I want is to be left alone. I am neither attracted
to you nor repelled by you. As far as I'm concerned,
you just don't exist—as a man, that is. Now can we get
down to business?'

He smiled. 'You can tell yourself that, Whitney, but
you really don't believe a word of it.'

'And how would you know what I believe?' Abruptly,
she realised that the portion of Kansas City that was
speeding by her window was one she had never seen
before. They were in a residential neighbourhood now,
and the only thing Whitney knew for certain was that it
was nowhere close to Country Club Plaza.

The sports car zipped past a school playground full
of children, paused at a stop-sign, and accelerated on to
a wide boulevard.

'Where are you taking me?' she demanded.

There was a wolfish twinkle in Max's eyes. 'Out to
see my house,' he said.

'Terrific,' Whitney muttered. A twinge of panic tingled
through her veins. I should have jumped out at the in-

53

tersection, she thought. No, there wasn't time. But if he stops again, I'm going to run. I'm old enough to know that it isn't residential architecture he wants to teach me about!

'Do you like old houses?' he asked politely. 'I thought perhaps you'd enjoy seeing this one. It was built as a brick farmhouse, one of the original settlers' homes. *Ante-bellum*, of course—it even has scars on the walls where the bullets hit it during the battle of Westport.'

All I need at the moment is a history lesson, Whitney thought. Where on earth did he get the idea that I wanted to rush right off and climb into bed with him? Surely I haven't given him any reason to believe that I'd welcome this sort of thing!

Men like Max, she thought acidly, didn't need any encouragement. They assumed automatically that any woman was not only available, but was delighted to receive their attentions. Well, Max Townsend was in for the surprise of his life. She'd show him that she was no silly innocent to be taken advantage of!

He swung the car into a long drive, slowing down as they approached a red-brick house. It looked a little like a wedding cake, Whitney thought idly, with a white-pillared veranda on three sides and two round-topped dormer windows peeking out of the roof.

'The porch was a later addition, of course,' Max said, waving a hand towards it. 'It's hard to believe that the house was originally very streamlined and plain, isn't it?' He didn't seem to expect an answer, which was just as well, because Whitney had lost track of her voice.

Attached to the back of the house was a low garage, with a door standing open to the autumn sunshine.

That's my best bet, Whitney thought. Get out of the car and run. Surely someone in the neighbourhood will help me.

But as the car eased to a stop, Max touched a button, and the garage door slid silently into place. The garage was dark, and Whitney was trapped.

She clenched her hands and said, low and fierce, 'I know, of course, why you brought me here.'

'You do?'

She turned on him. 'You won't get away with it, Max.'

'I won't?'

'No! I've told you I'm not interested in sleeping with you. Rape is rape, no matter where it happens——'

'Rape?' He sounded mildly confused. 'Oh, I see. You think I brought you here to—how did they describe it in the old days?—to have my evil way with you.'

Whitney swallowed hard. 'What else am I supposed to think?' she asked feebly.

'Oh, I could, of course,' he said thoughtfully, 'if you're quite determined on it. But I'm afraid the girls in the office would be embarrassed if I came through with you over my shoulder, screaming.'

'Office?' Whitney's voice was a croak.

'Yes. I rented a suite downtown for a while, but it wasn't very practical. I'm either out with the clients or working on the telephone, you see, so I was paying rent for space I never used, and doing my work at home. When I bought the house, I remodelled the lower floor into an office. It's very handy.' He smiled at her. 'I'm sorry if you're disappointed at not being ravished this morning, but we really have a lot of work to do.'

Whitney put her face down into her hands.

'I'll check with my secretary, though,' Max went on relentlessly. 'Perhaps I can pencil you in this afternoon some time.'

She swung out at him in blind rage. Max caught her wrist. 'Naughty, naughty,' he said pleasantly. 'We really are going to have to work on that temper of yours.'

If there had been a crack in the cement floor of the garage, Whitney would have crawled into it. 'I have made a prize fool of myself, haven't I?' she muttered.

Max was cheerful. 'That's one of the things that attracts me to you, Whitney,' he confided. 'There are too many women in the world who are always perfect. Neat as a pin, every hair in place, never visible without make-up, and socially rigid to boot. They never say the wrong thing, and they associate only with people who are just like them. Whereas you——'

'Please,' Whitney groaned. 'Don't rub it in.'

Max grinned and went on. 'They also have no sense of humour and they act remarkably like plastic dolls. I'm always expecting their mechanical voiceboxes to get stuck and leave them saying "How nice—— How nice—— How nice" till their batteries run down.'

It actually sounded as if he was giving her a compliment. Whitney thought about it, and asked, 'And do I have a sense of humour?'

'Of course you do. Some day you'll be telling someone about what happened today and you'll burst out laughing at your own ridiculous behaviour.'

'I wouldn't bet on it being any time soon.'

'I would.' He took her through a small passageway to what would have once been the basement of the old house. 'We're coming in the back way, of course,' he pointed out. 'The regular office entrance is at the side of the house, but this gives me a private escape route.'

'I see. That would be important to you, I'm sure.' She smiled innocently up at him.

'Of course it is,' he retorted. 'I live in the rest of the house, you know. I wouldn't like having to go out in the cold to get there.'

'But an office in the basement?' The idea was less than appealing.

Max shrugged. 'I didn't want to cut up the rest of the house. It does have some historic value.'

'I understand that, but still——' Whitney wrinkled her nose in expectation of darkness and gloom and a musty smell. How could anyone work in such conditions?

But she soon discovered her mistake. The room they stepped into was light and airy, with pale panelled walls, and carpeting that cushioned her feet. Along the opposite wall was a row of small desks, each surrounded by noise-absorbent panels. At two of them, young women were using telephones. The only clue that they were in a basement was the high windows that sprinkled sunshine across the room.

A receptionist looked up with a cheerful smile and handed Max a stack of pale yellow message slips. 'Good morning, Mrs Lattimer,' she said.

Whitney responded automatically, wondering how the woman had known her name. Then she saw Cindy Bell coming across the big room, the ever-present clipboard in hand, and reminded herself that all businesses had grapevines. Apparently Max's office was no exception. And neither was Tyler-Royale, she remembered. She had almost forgotten that Pete Ward had seen her with Max last night, and had jumped to an embarrassing conclusion. By this morning, the news could have reached the San Francisco store.

You might as well accept it, she told herself glumly. It's too late to stop it, that's sure.

'Hi, Max,' Cindy said. 'Good morning, Mrs Lattimer.'

Max looked up from his messages. 'Are you headed for the store?'

Cindy glanced at her watch. 'I've just got time to make it,' she warned. 'If you want any errands run this morning, you'll have to do them yourself.'

'No respect for authority,' Max grumbled. 'Actually, I want you to skip the regular routine and stay here. We'll start designing the interview questionnaire this morning, and you can test it this afternoon.'

'Can you put it together that quickly?' Whitney asked.

Max grinned. 'Once I make up my mind what I'm after, it never takes me very long to achieve the result.'

It didn't take a genius to see the double meaning in that. But even worse, Max had accompanied the words with a warmly assessing look. Whitney felt her face starting to colour.

Then she told herself briskly not to be silly. He was only joking, she thought, carrying on the teasing that had started in the car. It was his nature to banter about it, and to give every phrase a suggestive twist. It didn't mean anything.

Or did it, she asked herself uneasily. What if he really intended to pursue her? There were some men who found the thrill of the hunt to be the real excitement. To a man like that, her coldness might be an irresistible challenge.

Well it will do him no good, she thought. I'm not interested, and sooner or later he'll get the message.

'We'll need you in half an hour, Cindy,' Max added briskly. He ushered Whitney into a conference room, with half a dozen deep leather chairs pulled up around an oval table, and shut the door.

'And why won't we need Cindy for half an hour?' Whitney asked.

'You're still suspicious of my motives, aren't you?' Max handed her a cup of coffee. 'Admit it, Whitney. You're afraid I'm going to push a button somewhere and the table will unfold into a bed.'

She didn't dignify that with a comment. 'So what are we going to do instead?'

'Bring you up to date.'

'Interpret all the paperwork, you mean? It's still up at the hotel—we forgot to bring it along this morning.'

'It doesn't matter. I never let important papers out of my hands.'

She sipped her coffee and took a moment to think about that. 'Do you mean that those stacks of statistics you gave me last night were meaningless?'

'Not all of them.' He held a chair for her. 'But you must admit, if I'd given you just a dozen pages, you'd have read them over a tray from room-service and missed a very interesting evening. Let's get to work.'

Whitney groaned. 'If it wasn't for those papers, you wouldn't have come up to my room last night at all. And if you'd stayed in the parking lot where you belonged, Pete Ward and half the Tyler-Royale employees wouldn't be convinced by now that I'm sleeping with you. The place has a grapevine that's faster than a jungle telegraph.'

He nodded. 'I am partly to blame, that's true.'

'Partly?' She looked at him in genuine astonishment. 'What do you mean, partly?'

'And I've been giving that problem some serious thought.'

'I don't believe I'm going to like this.'

'If they're determined to think the worst of us anyway, then we might as well enjoy ourselves and——'

'No, Max.'

He sighed. 'If you say so.' He took a single sheet of paper from his jacket pocket and spread it out in front of her. 'Here's the way it works,' he said, and leaned over her shoulder to point out the first set of figures. His cheek was brushing her hair, and the vague scent of his aftershave tickled her nose. He had braced one hand on the back of her chair, so that his arm was almost encircling her.

And there is not one thing I can do about it, Whitney thought. If I ask him to move away from me, he'll just innocently inquire if it bothers me. And then what do I say? If I say no, it doesn't, then he'll think he has permission to keep treating me this way. And if I admit that it does upset me to have him so close——

Does it really bother me? she asked herself. Or is it just habit to object? In a way, it's actually rather pleasant to sit here this way...

And that's enough of that nonsense, Whitney Lattimer! she added roundly.

'Max,' she said. 'This wouldn't look too good if Cindy came in unexpectedly.' She turned her head and looked into his eyes, big and dark brown and less than six inches from hers. 'You are practically hugging me,' she pointed out, trying to keep her voice calm.

'Cindy understands these things. But I see what you mean.' Slowly, as if reluctantly, he withdrew the offending arm. 'I suppose we'd better be careful. It wouldn't help get the work done if the staff figured out that we're nuts about each other.'

Whitney closed her eyes briefly, in pain. If I had a hammer, she thought wildly, I'd murder him right now. And there isn't a woman alive who would condemn me, if she heard the whole story!

But after that, Max behaved himself. By the time the morning was over, the questionnaire was completed. If the first test of it got good results, then these questions would be asked of every customer leaving the Tyler-Royale store, as well as people stopped at random on the streets of the Plaza.

And then we'll know, Whitney thought. We'll know why they don't buy at Tyler-Royale. We'll know why our brand-new store is falling apart.

There was no doubt left in her mind now that Max was correct. It was fortunate that they were acting now, before the balance sheets showed a steady decline, instead of this minor flutter.

Soon, she thought, we'll know. And just as soon as we have the results, I can go home again.

It surprised her to realise that the thought of going home hadn't crossed her mind once during the morning. The longing to be in her own apartment must have simply been a side-effect of the jet-lag, she decided.

It was just as well, she thought, because she couldn't go home for a few days at least. It would take that long to get even the most preliminary results from the questionnaire. Max would push it along as much as he could, but the survey would be worthless if it wasn't skilfully taken and carefully analysed, and that could take weeks.

But she wouldn't have to be in Kansas City all that time, she decided. Once they had established some plan of action to get the store out of its immediate danger, and once Pete Ward understood it and began to carry it out, she would be free to leave. There would be future trips, of course, to check out the progress of the store. But once the survey was done, she wouldn't even have to check in with Max. The trips would be quick ones, then, surprise visits to be sure the store was operating well.

No more Max. That in itself, she told herself, would be a fringe benefit worth noting.

She glanced at the draft of the questionnaire on the table in front of her. It was the third version that Max's secretary had typed. This one was very rough yet, with words scratched out, phrases written in the margins, whole sentences replaced. The secretary would have a rough time finding her way through it all.

'We can't run this without warning Pete,' she said finally.

Max leaned back in his chair and chewed on the end of his pencil. 'Must you?'

'Don't be an idiot, Max. He has eyes. If twenty people abruptly show up in front of the store and start quizzing customers——'

'Even if you've given your permission?'

Whitney thought about it, and said reluctantly, 'I suppose I could tell him that we're doing this all over the country.'

Max shook his head. 'It would be too easy to prove that story wrong. Didn't you just tell me about the rumour-mill?'

'Then I'll tell him we're testing it here. It's true, you know. If this works, we could use it at every store.'

'Better. But don't say too much,' Max warned.

Whitney was exasperated. 'It sounds as if you think Pete is the problem!'

'I learned long ago never to underestimate the ability of a manager to mismanage.'

'Well, just remember, if you can, that Pete is on our side.' She glanced at her wristwatch. 'I'll call him now and take him to lunch.' Very neat, she congratulated herself. With one simple move, she had forestalled an invitation to lunch with Max, and she had started getting down to the real business.

The idea of losing her company for a meal didn't seem to bother Max. 'Use the phone in my office,' he suggested. 'I'll get this retyped for your final approval before you go.'

Funny, she thought as she dialled the store's number. She had half expected him to protest, and ask her to wait till after lunch to talk to Pete.

Don't be silly, she told herself. Max was a professional, after all. He would flirt with her in odd moments as long as it pleased him to do so, because it was in his nature to pursue any attractive woman who crossed his path; he had as much as told her that himself last night at dinner. But when it came to a choice between a woman and his work, Max would get down to business in a moment, and the woman would be history.

Her call took only moments to reach Pete Ward's secretary, but at that point it was like running into a brick wall. 'I'm sorry, Mrs Lattimer,' the woman said. 'Mr Ward is not here at the moment. I'll have him call you as soon as he returns.'

'I can't leave Max's number, Whitney thought. 'I'll be hard to reach,' she said. 'When should I call back?'

There was a hesitation, so brief that Whitney almost didn't notice it. Then the woman asked, 'May I tell him what it is in reference to?'

Whitney said gently, 'I thought you said he wasn't there.'

'Oh, he isn't! But if it's really important, I could try to reach him——'

And since when, Whitney asked herself, was it the secretary's job to decide what was really important? 'So you aren't expecting him back at all today?'

'No.'

There was nothing so very unusual about that, Whitney thought. Everybody took an afternoon off now and then. But there was something about the woman's voice—— She sounded guilty, Whitney concluded, as if she had somehow been caught at something shady.

'I'll check back later,' she said. 'Just in case he comes in.'

'I'll tell him you called.'

I'll just bet you will, Whitney thought as she cradled the phone. She wondered where Pete Ward was, and why the secretary hadn't wanted to tell her. Ross had never insisted that his managers punch a timeclock; they all worked whatever hours were necessary for the job. So even if Pete was taking advantage of a sunny morning to play golf, there would have been no objections from headquarters.

And the secretary thought I was calling from Chicago, Whitney thought. Wherever Pete Ward had got the information that had made him show up at the hotel last night, it hadn't been at the store, for the secretary obviously hadn't known that Whitney was in Kansas City. But Pete Ward knew. He apparently had concluded that her trip was purely personal, and that he had no cause to be careful. But if his secretary caught up with him and told him that Whitney had called——

That added a new dimension to the problem, and she thought about it for a few minutes, then got up and went in search of Max.

He pushed a copy of the finished questionnaire across the table towards her. Whitney looked at it idly and said, 'This looks fine.'

Max's eyebrows raised. Just a few minutes ago, he seemed to be thinking, when the previous draft had been given to her, she had inspected every comma. Now, she didn't seem to care.

'Can you take me up to the store now?' she asked abruptly.

'Sure. I'll have the copies run, and Cindy and I can start the test while you're breaking the news to Pete.'

'I meant right now,' Whitney said. 'Perhaps I'd better call a cab, then.'

'It's that important? I'll be ready to go in half an hour.'

She said, slowly, 'I don't know. It might be very important.'

'Do you drive?'

She nodded.

'Then take my car.'

She caught the set of keys he tossed to her. 'I promise to treat it with respect.'

'That's what scares me,' he murmured. The look in his eyes said that he expected never to see his car in one piece again.

The secretary was astounded when Whitney appeared in her office. 'Mrs Lattimer,' she sputtered. 'I had no idea you were actually here in the city——'

'Have you reached Mr Ward yet?' Whitney asked pleasantly. She searched her memory. Georgia, that was the woman's name.

'Why, no, I——'

'Give it another try, please, Georgia. I'll wait for him in his office.'

'But he doesn't like anyone to be in there——'

'And where else would you suggest that I work?' She didn't give the secretary a chance to think of another excuse to keep her out.

With the office door safely closed behind her, Whitney leaned against it and surveyed the room. Pete Ward had done himself proud here, she decided. It was a pleasant room, with dark wood-panelled walls, plush carpeting, a huge walnut desk. The desk-top contained a blotter, a pen in a stand, a calendar, a double picture-frame, and nothing else. Peter Ward had always been neat, she remembered, right down to the pictures of his wife and kids on his desk, which he updated twice a year.

'A clean desk indicates an organised mind,' Whitney murmured. Who was it who had said that? And who had said the opposite—that a clean desk meant an empty mind? She wondered which was correct in Pete Ward's case.

She sat down in his big leather chair. It tipped back almost automatically, as if it was often in that position. She looked at the calendar. There was nothing written on it. She flipped through the pages and found the last entry, made nearly two weeks before. There was nothing on the blotter, not an idle phone number nor a doodle. But the picture frame didn't hold the expected photos. Instead, there were two arty shots of a very beautiful, wide-eyed young woman. In fact, she was young enough to be Pete Ward's daughter, Whitney thought, except for the minor problem that Pete's children were both boys.

'Well, well,' Whitney said, and picked up the telephone as the intercom buzzed.

'I can't find Mr Ward,' the secretary said. She sounded subdued.

'I'll be happy to wait while you keep trying,' Whitney said cordially. 'In the meantime, would you ring Women's Sportswear for me, please?'

She tapped her pen on the blotter. 'Sportswear, Karen Emerson,' a warm voice said.

When she heard the name, Whitney smiled. 'Hello, Karen.'

'Whitney!' The young buyer sounded delighted.

Whitney picked up the picture-frame and studied the face of the girl in the photograph. 'How would you like to come up and tell me everything you know about this store?' she asked.

'Sorry, dear. It's a busy time, and I can't possibly come to Chicago right now. Next week, perhaps. What do you want to know, anyway?'

'The grapevine must be falling apart.' Whitney turned the chair away from the desk and inspected the painting on Pete Ward's wall. 'I didn't mean Chicago.'

'You're in town?'

'Right upstairs in Pete's office.'

'You mean Pete's there?'

Karen sounded sceptical, and Whitney tapped her pencil thoughtfully on the blotter. Now just what, she wondered, did that mean?

'I'll take you to lunch, if you'd rather. Not here, though—I want to be able to talk to you.'

Karen sighed. 'I'd love that. But I'm unpacking a shipment right now, and I can't leave.'

'Then we'll make it dinner.'

'Good. I'm even free for a change. My boyfriend is working late tonight. And Whitney?' Karen sounded hesitant. 'I'm glad you're here. There is something seriously wrong in this store. Nobody talks to each other any more, but there is an ear listening around every corner.'

Whitney sighed. 'I know, Karen. We're going to do something about that.' She turned the chair back towards the room, and looked up to see Pete Ward standing just inside the office door, arms folded across his chest. He looked furious.

'What in the hell is the meaning of this?' he blustered. 'You told me last night you were here for personal reasons, not business. Now I find you in my office, going through my drawers, snooping through my papers——'

Whitney's first instinct was to defend herself. She had not said her trip was personal. She had not been going through his desk, though she supposed that, strictly speaking, she had snooped through his calendar. But she forced that impulse down. To defend herself would only get them into a futile argument.

She leaned back in the chair instead, and looked up at Pete. What she would like to do, she thought, was to stand up and hammer on the desk and demand an explanation of the trouble. But something in his eyes stopped her. There was something under the bluster and the fury. Was it fear?

Compassion flooded through her. Whatever was wrong at Tyler-Royale's Kansas City store, Pete Ward was a human being, and he deserved to be treated humanely.

'This store is on the brink of failing,' she said. It wasn't harsh or cold, just factual. 'What went wrong, Pete?'

He could hear the compassion in her voice, that was obvious. All the bluster drained out of him, and he sank into a chair across from her. 'It's my fault,' he said. 'It's all my fault.'

And then, to Whitney's horror, he began to sob.

CHAPTER FIVE

'YOU only got here the day before yesterday,' Max said, as he set her suitcase down at the flight desk. 'I still don't see why you have to fly back to Chicago tonight.'

'Because I don't have a car, so I can't drive. Non-smoking, please,' Whitney told the clerk. She was darned if she would stand here and explain to Max just why it was important that she be on this flight. In fact, it hadn't been her idea to tell him about it at all. He had simply arrived at the hotel while she had been packing, to take her to dinner. The announcement that she was leaving had not discouraged Max. Neither had the idea that she had already called a cab. So here she was at the airport, with Max in tow.

He persisted. 'What I meant was, why can't you just call Ross and tell him what you've found out?'

'Because I'd rather talk to him in person.'

'But today when you went up to the store to talk to Pete, you had no intention of leaving——'

She picked up her boarding pass and turned to face him in exasperation. 'All right, Max. I'll give you the unvarnished truth. I'm going back to Chicago because I am completely out of clothes!'

'Now that explanation sounds like you.' He picked up her carry-on.

'Max, has anyone ever told you that you're just like Chinese water torture?' He never gave up and he never relented, she thought, and eventually everyone around him crumbled.

He thought it over. 'No, but I'll take it as a compliment.'

'Believe me, it wasn't intended that way. You don't need to walk me to the gate. I can get there by myself.'

68

He ignored her. 'I could go along and help explain it to Ross.'

'Explain what?'

'Oh, I could tell him about the questionnaire results. He'll appreciate the test-run.'

'Thanks, Max. But you don't even know why I'm going.'

'That's not my fault. I've spent the last hour trying to find out.'

'Personnel problems are none of your business, Max.'

'So it is Pete Ward,' he said cheerfully. 'How did a guy like that get a store of his own, anyway?'

Whitney stopped. 'What do you mean, a guy like that?'

'Just a hunch. In the six months he's been here, I've never run into him anywhere. It seemed a bit odd, that's all. Public relations is part of his job.'

'You could have told me that before.'

'Why? You wouldn't have believed me.'

She didn't argue; he was probably right. 'Pete showed promise as a department head at the Chicago store, so Ross promoted him. We're short of management people right now.'

Max shook his head. 'I warned Ross about this expansion programme of his. I told him he was moving too fast.'

'I'll pass along that charming endorsement of his executive decisions,' Whitney said sweetly. 'Goodbye, Max. Thanks for all your help.'

He raised an eyebrow. 'Why do I get the idea that you're saying farewell for ever?'

'Oh, I'll be back now and then to check on the store, but my job here is done as soon as I make my report to Ross. Don't take it personally, Max.'

'Do you have to sound so delighted about it?'

'Did I?' Whitney assessed her own mood, and decided that she really wasn't pleased at all. It was going to be no fun to explain her findings to Ross, and persuade him that she was right about Pete Ward. Besides, there were moments of this trip that had been rather enjoyable. 'Look, I have to board the plane now,' she pointed out. 'I'm sure Ross will call you about the details.'

'Checking up on you? He's a wiser man than I thought.' Max draped the strap on her carry-on bag across her shoulder.

The sudden weight reminded Whitney of the hundreds of miles she must have walked through airport terminals all over the world, carrying that bag. She sighed. 'Sometimes I think if I never see another aeroplane it will be too soon for me.'

Max's hands gripped her shoulders and spun her easily around to face him. Warm fingers crept up her throat to caress her cheek.

Startled, Whitney looked up into his eyes, which were darker than she had ever seen them before. That's a nice trick, she thought idly. It makes him look very sincere. I wonder how he does it.

'Don't go,' he said. 'Stay with me.' He didn't wait for an answer. Instead, he kissed her. It was a careful caress at first—as if he were sampling a new dessert—but Whitney quickly forgot things like eyes and aeroplanes. His hand slipped to the nape of her neck, holding her against him, and the terminal began to revolve around her.

Whitney was half-dizzy and starting to feel queasy when she broke away from him. 'I can't,' she said, and her voice was small and tight. 'I can't.'

Max sighed. 'I know,' he said. 'But this isn't the end.'

It has to be, Whitney told herself. It is the end. I can't do this, not ever again. It scares me too much——

He kissed the tip of her nose, gently. 'Call me when you get to Chicago,' he said.

She nodded, only half hearing him, and turned blindly towards the clerk, holding out her boarding-pass. The woman glanced at it, and then looked over Whitney's shoulder to where Max was disappearing down the corridor. 'Lucky girl,' she murmured, with a twinge of envy in her voice.

Whitney's breathing still hadn't straightened out by the time she reached her seat. Her breath was coming in sharp little gasps that felt like ice-cubes, cold and hard with corners that stabbed her. She sank into her seat and put a hand over her eyes.

My God, she thought, horrified and heartsick at her own reactions. She had stood there in the terminal and allowed Max to kiss her like a lover.

Which is precisely what he was after, she told herself wearily. He had made no effort to disguise what he wanted from her; he had even announced that he intended to make love to her. So why should she be upset about that kiss?

He wasn't going to succeed in his intention, that was sure. She had made up her mind long ago that she would never become involved with another man, certainly not with one like Max. Even Ross—his best friend—had called Max a ladies' man.

But she was very glad that Max hadn't realised what she meant when she had choked out, 'I can't.' He had thought she merely meant that she couldn't cancel her trip. It would be just as well that it remained that way, she told herself. She would just have to be more careful to keep control of herself in the future, and not let Max put her in that kind of position again. She would make sure she was never alone with him——

And what good would that do, she asked herself. If he didn't hesitate to kiss her like that in the airport terminal, he wasn't likely to draw the line at any other public place either. She wouldn't be safe, no matter where she went.

And that, Whitney Lattimer, she told herself sharply, is one of the stupidest ideas you've ever come up with. Unsafe, indeed! Max had said that he seldom travelled any more. He certainly wouldn't come pounding up to

Chicago to pursue a reluctant Whitney. There were plenty of women, far more willing than she, who would be delighted to keep him occupied.

Feeling relieved, she put her head back and tried to go to sleep. And if her relief was mixed with just a tinge of regret, Whitney chose not to recognise it.

Ross was waiting for her at O'Hare. 'I'm sorry to drag you away from the baby,' she said.

He kissed her cheek and took her bags. 'That's all right,' he said. 'Kelly kicked me out of her hospital room anyway. She said I was keeping her awake and she'll need all her strength tomorrow when she brings young Andrew home.'

'Already?'

'What do you mean, already? He's more than a day old and he's still hanging around the nursery. I tell you, Whitney, we're raising a generation of malingerers.'

'You're raising them,' Whitney pointed out. 'I'm not.'

Ross shook his head. 'I still have hopes that some day——'

'Please stop doing the big-brother stuff, Ross. That's not what I came home to talk to you about.'

'I didn't think your important news included an announcement that you'd got married while you were away. Your apartment, I presume?'

'Yes. I'd like to collapse in my own bed for a change.' She yawned.

'Oh?' Ross was pleasantly inquisitive. 'Just whose bed have you been collapsing in?'

'Please, Ross, I only meant that I was tired of hotel rooms.'

'You must be more careful to make yourself clear.'

'You and Max have so much in common. You even think the same way.' She tried to fight off another yawn, and failed. 'You won't be in the office tomorrow, then?'

'I wasn't planning to come in. But if you don't want to talk about it now——'

'Let's get it out of the way tonight.'

'Good. I'm dying of curiosity. What was so important that you couldn't tell me over the phone?'

'Let's wait till we're home, all right? I want your full attention to be on me, not on the expressway.'

'If you insist. How is Max, by the way?'

Whitney darted a look at him. Had there been an odd note in his question?

Ross raised an eyebrow. 'You know—Max? You've met and all? You did mention him a moment ago, or was it only my imagination?'

'Don't be sarcastic, Ross. I'm exhausted.' She put her head back against the seat. By city standards, traffic was light on the expressway, and in record time Ross was pulling the car into the parking-garage under the tower where Whitney rented a small apartment. As the lift whisked them upwards, Ross said, 'I gather that you and Max didn't hit it off?'

'That's a safe guess. To answer your question, Max is fine, and as much as I hate to admit it, he was even right. The store is in trouble.'

'How big?'

Whitney fumbled for her key, and the memory of Max opening the suite door stabbed at her. The look on Pete Ward's face had been something to remember, she thought with a secret little smile. Max had carried it off with distinction, as if he did it every day.

And he probably did, too, she reminded herself, with one woman or another! She put the memory firmly behind her and stepped into her apartment. She kicked off her shoes, turned on the lights, and tossed herself down into a chair.

'Whitney?' Ross reminded. 'We were talking about the store.'

'The first thing you have to do is get Pete Ward out of there.'

Ross whistled soundlessly.

'For the store's sake, and for Pete,' she went on. 'Did you know that his wife refused to move to Kansas City with him?'

'No. I'd heard that their marriage was on the rocks, but——'

'That was why.'

'He never said a word about it to me. In fact, he jumped at the opportunity to get his own store.'

'He told me about that. You offered him the job, and he accepted with delight. Then he went home and told his wife that they were moving to Kansas City, and she laid down the law. He told me that you'd put so much faith in him that he couldn't disappoint you by backing out, so he went in spite of her.'

'That's just terrific,' Ross muttered. 'Am I so hard to stand up to?'

'Of course you are. You're an overbearing swine sometimes, Ross,' Whitney said sweetly. 'The first thing you'll have to do is get Pete back to Chicago and send him to a counsellor who'll teach him to say no.'

'To me or his wife?'

'Preferably both. Also to little dolls half his age who are looking for a big daddy, and to employees who like to stretch their coffee-breaks instead of taking care of customers, and——'

'You're actually serious?' Ross sounded stunned. 'I have a store that's failing because the manager can't say no?'

'That seems to be a good part of it. There is no discipline in that store.' She shifted uncomfortably in her chair. 'Would you mind waiting while I change clothes? I feel as if I've been wearing this suit for three weeks.'

'Only if you don't care if I raid your kitchen.'

'Good luck. If the cleaning lady didn't remember her promise, you will find only mould.'

When she came back to the kitchen a few minutes later, comfortable in a sloppy sweatshirt and jeans, Ross was inspecting the refrigerator.

'What you're really telling me,' he said, 'is that I should consider getting rid of Pete altogether. Am I right?'

Whitney sighed. 'No, I think he's salvageable. He was wonderful as a department head, and he could be again.'

'Not if he can't say no.'

'I think he just got out of his depth, Ross. Having the responsibility of the whole store frightened him. And being without his wife didn't help. According to Karen Emerson—do you remember Karen?'

Ross nodded. He was munching on a wholewheat cracker.

'Karen says the little sweetheart he's been dating has charged thousands of dollars' worth of clothes to Pete's employee account. She questioned it, and he approved the charges.'

'He doesn't just need a counsellor, Whitney, he needs a shrink.'

'Perhaps. But if you fire him, you'll never get paid for the clothes,' she pointed out brightly.

'Does he really want to break that off?'

'He says so. I believe that he means it. It'll be easier, of course, if he isn't in Kansas City.'

'I'm not convinced. You've only heard his side of it, Whitney.'

'Pete admits that he was a fool, Ross. But it isn't entirely his fault. He couldn't make it as a manager, that's all.'

'As far as that goes,' Ross said thoughtfully, 'the department could certainly stand having him back. It's been on a slide since he left.'

She smiled up at him. 'So it's all settled. Pete will come back here, to the job he loved and did well. Perhaps he and his wife will even patch it up.'

'Hold it, Whitney,' Ross warned. 'Don't be a do-gooder. And I haven't made any promises yet.'

'I know I'm being realistic, you'll see. You should have seen the man, Ross. He was really heartbroken about what had happened to his store, and he didn't know how to go about fixing it.'

'Somehow,' Ross murmured, 'Pete Ward sounds less than sincere.'

'You weren't there. I was. Would you like an omelette, or would you prefer to finish off the crackers?'

'Do I have to choose?' He bit into another cracker. 'They both sound good. Pete could have come to see me when he started getting into trouble, you know.'

'He was scared of what you'd say. He didn't want to disappoint you, and he thought he could turn things around. Instead, they kept getting worse. Actually, Ross, I think he was almost glad to see me.'

Ross made a sound half-way between a sigh and a grunt. 'And you really think that moving Pete will solve the problem in Kansas City?'

Whitney shrugged. 'It will go a long way towards it. At least bring Pete back here and listen to his story before you fire him.'

'All right. But what about the store?'

She started breaking eggs into a bowl. 'Put a good, solid manager in there, and he can have the place shipshape in a couple of months. Pete has lost the respect of the staff; he couldn't regain it now no matter what he tried. But another manager could come in——'

'Who?'

'Someone with experience. That was the mistake last time. A new store shouldn't have a new manager.'

'Granted. It was a bad mistake, and I won't make it again. But who do you suggest I transfer? I don't exactly have management personnel lined up outside my office waiting for me to snap my fingers.'

'Why are you asking me?' Whitney said from the depths of a cupboard, where she was searching for the omelette pan. 'A brand-new store, in an urban location—they'll jump at it.'

Ross took the pan out of her hand and helped her up. 'I'm asking you because you're the one who has the firm ideas of what the store needs. So how about an answer to my question? Who gets the job?'

Whitney shrugged. 'Jim Higgins is great. Or Joe Loomis could whip it into shape. Or Craig Hunter. You've got a dozen possibilities.'

'Higgins, Loomis, and Hunter all have stores and are settled,' Ross pointed out. 'They also have houses, wives, and families. I can't ask any of them to start work in Kansas City by next Monday—it wouldn't be fair to them.'

'You'll have to.' Whitney poured the egg mixture into the pan and watched as it started to sizzle. 'A store in trouble can't run itself for a month while one of those guys sells a house and moves. Especially not with the Christmas season coming up fast.'

'Oh, I couldn't agree with you more,' Ross said blandly. 'You might want to take your car this time. You'll probably need transport.'

'Where am I going?' She tipped the omelette pan gently and looked up at him, puzzled.

'To Kansas City.'

'Why would I be—no, Ross.'

'You're the only skilled manager I have who isn't tied to a store at the moment, Whitney. And you don't have a house or a family.'

'I don't have a wife, either, but I fail to see what that's got to do with anything. Ross, I am not going back to Kansas City.'

'See?' Ross asked plaintively. 'I told you I'm not hard to say no to. You've done it twice in two minutes. Now, when are you leaving?'

An hour later, Whitney gave up in despair. Ross had been perfectly pleasant, agreeable, and charming, as well as absolutely immovable.

'That's the way it is, Whitney,' he said. 'It's you, or it's no one at all. I'll have you back out of there just as soon as I can get another manager moved in. But in the meantime——'

He was right, she knew. There was no other choice, save letting the store slide even further into turmoil.

'Why don't you hire Max and put him to work?' she said finally, sarcastically.

'I've tried. He's too fond of being his own boss.'

'That's the trouble with efficiency experts,' Whitney grumbled. 'They never do any of the work themselves. They just tell everybody else how to.'

'I wish I knew what you have against Max.' He glanced at his watch and carried their empty plates to the dishwasher. 'So when will you be taking over the store?'

'Can I at least pick up my mail and send my clothes to the cleaners before I leave again?'

'Sure. Take a couple of days, if you need to.' He ruffled her hair. 'You won't be there any more than a month, Whitney. I promise I'll have a new manager in by then.'

Famous last words, she thought. 'Did you and Max cook this idea up together?'

There was no mistaking the look of astonishment on Ross's face. 'Why on earth should we?' he asked.

Whitney felt like an idiot for voicing the suspicion. 'It was just a thought.'

'Well, get rid of it. I'm running a business for profit, not a dating service for Max Townsend.'

'Be sure you tell Max that.' She said a meek goodbye, promised to visit the next day to admire the new baby, and closed the door behind him with a deceptively calm click.

'But I don't want to go back to Kansas City!' she wailed in the silent living-room.

There was, however, no point in continuing to argue against fate. So she unpacked her bags, sorted her clothes into piles for the laundry and the cleaners, and finally fell into bed. She was thinking, as she lay there, that time spent between her own fragrant sheets would be so rare in the next few weeks that she shouldn't waste any of it in sleeping. It was illogical, she knew. But before she could figure out where the flaw in the logic lay, she had fallen asleep.

The telephone woke her. She fumbled for it, and saw that the bedside clock stood at precisely one in the morning. 'What idiot is on the phone at this hour?' she moaned as she picked it up.

'You said you'd call me,' a masculine voice accused.

'Max.' She lay back against her piled pillows and closed her eyes. 'At least that answers my question.'

'What question?'

'Never mind. What do you want? And how did you get this number?'

'I wanted to be sure you'd got there all right. So I woke Ross up and requested the necessary information.'

'And after Ross told you that I was safely on the ground and securely barricaded in my apartment, you called me anyway? Do you know what time it is?'

'It's eight in the morning in Paris,' he said cheerfully. 'We could be sightseeing.'

'Don't you ever sleep?'

'Not any more than necessary. It's a waste of time. What I really called for——'

'Good. Let's get down to business so I can go back to sleep.'

'——was to tell you that I'll be in Detroit on business the week after next. I could stop in Chicago and take you to dinner and a show. If you'd like it, that is.'

'Can't.' Whitney yawned. 'I won't be in town.'

There was a momentary silence. Then he accused, 'I haven't even told you which days I could be there.'

'It doesn't matter.'

'Oh, I see. I'm getting the brush-off.'

'Not exactly.' He'll find out sooner or later, she thought. I might as well bite the bullet and tell him myself. 'I'll be in Kansas City. I'm the new manager of the Tyler-Royale store. Only temporarily, I might add, until Ross transfers someone.'

Max's voice warmed. 'That's even better. How long will we have?'

'You needn't clear all the other women out of your appointment book to keep me happy, Max. I'm coming down to work.'

She could almost see his shrug. 'You can't work all the time.'

'I'm going to try. The faster I get that store in shape, the sooner Ross can get someone else in there.'

'What would Ross do if he didn't have you?'

'I haven't any idea. Some day I may resign and find out.'

'Haven't you ever wanted to do anything else?'

'Besides work for Tyler-Royale? Of course not. My great-grandfather Tyler established it, my grandfather built it into a chain, my mother still plays with being chairman of the board, when she isn't on the Riviera. What else is there for me to do?'

'You've never, ever, thought of doing something else?'

'What is this, a job interview? Where shall I send a copy of my C.V.?' She gave up and curled in a ball on her side, the telephone squeezed between her ear and the pillow. 'Yes, as a matter of fact, I have. I always wanted to start a unique little operation that specialised in the unusual. You want it, come in and tell us about it. We'll get it for you, no matter where we have to go to find it. If you need a different sort of gift, we've got it. The more unusual it is, the better we like it.'

'So why don't you do it?'

'Be practical, Max. Do you know what I'd have to charge?'

'People will pay anything for service these days.'

'Don't bet on it.' Her voice was soft as she went on. 'I'd call it "Heart's Desire"—because you could buy your fondest dream there.'

'It would be exclusive, of course.'

'That's part of the charm. Run a market survey, Max, and when you find the right location let me know.'

'You're teasing, aren't you?'

'Of course. It isn't feasible.'

'You really hate the travel, don't you, Whitney?'

'I've got used to it.'

'That doesn't answer the question. You don't have to keep it up, you know.'

'And how do you suggest that I avoid it? Ross got married and quit. I don't plan to follow in his footsteps.'

'Never?'

'Nope.' She yawned again. 'Once a person has been married——' Her voice trailed off. She knew what she wanted to say, but her tongue wasn't willing to shape the words right.

'He must have been quite a guy,' Max said softly.

There was no answer.

'Whitney?'

A long sigh and a sleepy murmur was the only reply.

Whitney stretched and opened her eyes to sunshine spilling in through the windows that looked out over Lake Michigan. The stretch dislodged the telephone, which bounced on the carpet. She reached down for it, a puzzled look on her face, and then remembered.

'Good grief!' she murmured. 'I fell asleep while I was talking to him. Poor Max.'

She was about to hang it up when a voice said, clearly, 'Good morning, Whitney.'

'Max? You're still here?'

'Of course.'

'Your phone bill is going to look like the national debt.'

'You've never seen my bill. This won't even cause a flutter in it.'

'Do you mean you really kept this line open all this time? Whatever for?'

'Because it was the only way I could think of, on the spur of the moment, to spend the night with you.'

That sounded like Max. She was momentarily speechless.

'Besides, I've found out all kinds of things,' he added cheerfully. 'I now know that you snore, for instance.'

Whitney was incensed. 'I do not!'

'You most certainly do. It's a cute little snore, too. And you talk in your sleep.'

She swallowed hard. Dignity would have kept her silent, but curiosity won out. 'What did I say?'

'Nothing intelligible, I'm afraid. But it was very sexy to listen to.'

'You sat there all night and listened to me sleep?'

'Of course not.' It was some relief, but he promptly removed it. 'I didn't sit. Do you think you're the only person in the world with a bedside phone?'

'This is an invasion of privacy, Max.'

'Tell you what. I'll take you to dinner the first night you're back and we'll argue it out then. All right? Unless you'd rather have breakfast together right now. I could go and get my crispy cereal and pour the milk on carefully so you could hear——'

'Goodbye, Max!' She slammed the phone down on his laughter.

She drew her knees up under the sheet, put her elbows on them, and propped her chin on her hands. Max Townsend was a danger to the entire female population, she decided. What kind of degenerate would call up a woman and then spend the night listening to her sleep?

A romantic one. The thought crept in from the back corner of her mind, and Whitney banished it. 'There isn't a romantic bone in Max Townsend's body,' she said to the room at large. 'He's a Don Juan, and any woman who comes close to him deserves whatever she gets!'

Why, she wondered sadly, did all men want to take advantage of any woman who came along? Why did all men have to be like Charles, blind to the needs of the women around them?

All men except Ross, of course. His wife was a rare, lucky woman.

She pushed back the blankets and padded across the bedroom to find some clothes. On her empty suitcase lay two bedraggled pink roses. She picked one up and smelled it. She had felt silly to be bringing them home with her, and yet she somehow hadn't wanted to abandon them in the impersonal hotel room, either.

She stood there and sniffed the wilted rose, and wondered about Max. Just where, she thought, did Max fit in?

CHAPTER SIX

WHITNEY signed a letter with a flourish and reached for the next one. 'You've done a good job on these, Georgia,' she told the secretary. They looked neat and precise, just the way a Tyler-Royale letter should, and the secretary deserved praise, despite the fact that it had taken her two tries to get them right.

Georgia nodded stiffly. She still looked a little irritated, as if to say that the first bunch of letters had been quite as acceptable. Whitney didn't try to persuade her; either Georgia would learn how Whitney operated, or there would soon be a new face in the outer office. She rather thought Georgia would learn. It had only been a few hours since Whitney had officially moved into the manager's office. She was willing to give Georgia some time to adjust.

A flashing light on the telephone caught the secretary's attention. 'Shall I answer that here, Mrs Lattimer?' she asked.

Whitney nodded and began to read a memo that would soon be distributed to the whole staff. She only half heard the conversation; it wasn't until Georgia told the caller for the second time that the manager was too busy to be bothered that Whitney looked up.

'I am perfectly able to take calls,' she said pointedly.

'Would you hold a moment, please?' Georgia pushed a button. 'I know, Mrs Lattimer,' she said, 'but it's only this old lady complaining about her confectionery again. Mr Ward talked to her—there's no sense in her wasting your time.'

Whitney pushed her chair back from the desk, and said, carefully keeping her voice even, 'I shall never be too busy to talk to a customer who has a complaint,

Georgia. If I'm not here, then I'll call back, but I shall talk to every person who telephones me.'

Georgia blinked. 'Yes, ma'am,' she said. There was a note in her voice that added, and you'll be sorry about that decision!

Whitney took the telephone from the secretary's hand. 'This is Whitney Lattimer,' she said. 'I understand you wish to speak to me.'

'And who are you?' It was an old voice, a little quavery.

'I'm the store manager.'

'I've talked to the manager. He's a man,' the voice announced triumphantly.

'Mr Ward was here for several months. But I've recently taken his place.' So recently, she added to herself, that not even all my staff know about it, unless they saw me come in this morning. She pushed the memo across the desk to Georgia with a nod, and noticed as Georgia left the room that the secretary was trying to hide a smile.

I wonder which of the troublemakers I'm talking to, Whitney thought. Every store had a few, and obviously Georgia knew that this was one of them. I wonder if I should have spent more time talking to Pete, instead of telling him to get his bags packed and head right back to Chicago.

'Oh.' The elderly voice sounded slightly disappointed. 'Well, I'm Emma Meadows, and it's about my horehound drops. I used to get 'em at the general store when I was a girl. That's why I was so pleased when your store opened and I could get 'em again. I buy a quarter of a pound every time I come in. Once a week, when I do my shopping. Wednesdays.' She paused, as if thinking about it, and added firmly, 'Unless it rains, of course. I can't stand and wait at the bus-stop in the rain any more. It makes my rheumatism flare up. In bad weather I have to come on Thursdays. I don't like that at all. There are too many people down there on Thursdays.'

Whitney cut in neatly, before this unknown caller could start the rundown of her weekly itinerary. 'And there's been a problem with the horehound drops?'

'You might say,' Emma Meadows quavered. 'First they told me they were out. Then they said they were ordered.'

Whitney untangled the pronouns, and concluded that there were no horehound drops to be found in the store. 'The people in the confectionery department, you mean?'

'Who else would I have been talking to about my drops?' the old lady asked querulously. 'For a month this went on, with one excuse after another. Two weeks ago Wednesday—or was it Thursday? Did it rain that Wednesday?'

Whitney's head was starting to ache.

'Well, no matter. They told me that the factory had stopped making them. Now what am I going to do?'

No wonder Georgia considered the woman a nut, Whitney thought. Most people would. Few would understand how important a tiny luxury like a quarter-pound of sweets, hoarded to last a whole week, could be to a lonely old lady.

'Mrs Meadows——'

'Miss,' the old voice said uncompromisingly.

I'm not surprised, Whitney thought. 'I'm sorry, Miss Meadows. I don't know the answer to your question right now,' Whitney said. 'But I shall investigate, and I'll call you back within a few minutes. Will you give me your number?' She jotted it down on the blotter, said goodbye, and sat for a moment biting her lip before reaching for her list of intercom numbers. 'We'll see what the department head has to say about it,' she murmured. Then she thought better of it and descended two levels to visit the department in person.

The department was small, but it appealed to the eye, with its rainbow of colours, and to the nose, with the delicious mix of aromas. I could gain ten pounds by just standing here inhaling, Whitney thought. She waited for the man behind the counter to weigh out two pounds of sculptured Italian chocolate, and then asked him about Emma Meadows.

She had got no further than the name before the man laughed heartily. 'So Old Maid Emma is at it again,' he said.

Whitney said icily, 'Miss Meadows has a complaint. I'm investigating it.'

'Mrs Lattimer, the woman has pestered us for weeks about those smelly drops. She was the only person who ever went near them, and——'

'But you did have them in stock?'

'Sure. And now we're out.'

'And you chose not to restock? They are still available?'

'Sure. At least, I guess so.'

'Why didn't you order more?'

'Be realistic, Mrs Lattimer. It took her six months to buy out our original stock, and it was the only thing she ever bought. A quarter of a pound of candy a week doesn't keep this store in business, and I can't afford to tie up counter-space with merchandise that doesn't move.'

Whitney thought fleetingly about pushing the man's nose into the nearest batch of soft fudge. 'At the moment, this store can't afford to lose a customer of any kind,' she said.

'Have you ever seen old Emma?'

Obviously the man wasn't good at taking hints. All right, Whitney thought, I'll spell it out. 'If you are wise,' she said, 'you will in the future refer to customers in an appropriate manner. Miss Meadows deserves as much respect as you are capable of showing.'

The man sighed. 'Sure, if you say so. But just wait till you see her. She always wears black, and it looks as if it hasn't been cleaned in a century——'

'I can't imagine why you think that should make a difference in the way she is treated,' Whitney said. 'Now, here's what you will do. You will order ten pounds of horehound drops from your supplier.'

'Are you ordering me to tie up counter-space with that stuff?'

'I didn't say that. You don't have to display the drops, if you don't have room. But you will have it on hand for Miss Meadows, at all times.'

The man groaned.

Whitney ignored him and went on. 'When they arrive, you will package two pounds of drops and send them to Emma Meadows, compliments of Tyler-Royale.'

'You don't make a profit that way,' he grumbled.

'You don't make one by turning customers away, either.' She looked him over, carefully. 'No,' she said, 'On second thoughts, you'll bring the parcel to me, and I'll mail it.'

'This is ridiculous.' It was muttered under his breath.

Whitney tapped a finger on the glass counter-top. 'And if it ever happens again,' she said, her patience exhausted, 'not only will I charge the drops to your personal account, but I'll take you out there with me and we'll deliver it. Got it, buster?'

'Got it.' He sounded sullen.

'Good.' She smiled. 'Now that we've established who's the boss, I think we'll get along just fine together.'

'Oh, you're the boss, all right.' It was a sarcastic grumble. 'Mrs Lattimer, ma'am, shall I salute?'

Whitney kept smiling. 'Not at all,' she said. 'I'm not the boss either, you see. Miss Meadows is. She and every other single customer who walks into this store. And if they don't like how we do our job, they're going to fire us all. Think about that, next time you weigh out a quarter of a pound of horehound drops.'

Her first employee meeting, with the buyers and the heads of each department, went well. So well, in fact, that Whitney had her fingers crossed under the table as she finished her pep-talk. 'We're on probation,' she said bluntly. 'If this store doesn't make a turn-around soon, it will be closed.'

A young man towards the back of the room said, 'Excuse me, Mrs Lattimer. But don't all new stores lose money? How can the head office invest in a building and stock if they expect to get it back in six months or a year?'

'We don't expect to earn back the capital investment in a few months,' Whitney said, 'or even in a few years. But neither do we expect that any store is going to lose money for more than the first few months of operation. Within a year of a store's opening, we expect to see it paying its own overheads—breaking even, in other words. After that, it should be making a profit. This one isn't doing that; in fact, it's going in the other direction.' Her throat was getting dry; she stopped and took a sip from the glass of water beside her. 'In addition, the head office has to consider the rest of the chain. One Tyler-Royale store getting a bad reputation for service will reflect on every other store around the country.'

There were nods around the table and a few murmurs.

'I know this is unpalatable news,' Whitney went on. 'It's not pleasant for any of us to think about the possibility that this store may close. But it isn't a threat, it's a fact. This store is in danger. We've already started a crash programme to find out precisely what is wrong. In the meantime, it's extremely important for each of us to pamper every customer we have left. It's something like a back garden—if you lose half of your plants to a frost, you don't ignore the other half and hope they'll grow. You give them extra attention, baby them, nurse them along.'

She put her notebook down and dusted the chalk smears off her hands. 'I've given you a picture of a sinking ship, today. If any of you are tempted to jump off it in an effort to save your own careers, I hope you'll come and talk to me before you make any decisions. I have every confidence that we can patch this boat up and make it seaworthy again—but not if we only stand on the deck and cry about it.'

There was a smattering of applause. Whitney's eyebrows went up, but she didn't comment. There was a buzz of conversation as the group straggled out of the conference room, a far cry from the dead silence that had fallen when she came in.

Karen Emerson paused beside Whitney. 'Good job, Coach,' she murmured. 'They liked you.'

'I really don't care about that,' Whitney said. 'The important thing is, did they believe me?'

'Oh, yes. Of course, Miss Meadows' horehound drops didn't hurt you.' Karen laughed at the quizzical expression on Whitney's face. 'The grapevine is back in order. That story had hit all three floors by the time you got back to your office.'

'Well, I hope no one thinks that I only did it for the effect.'

'They don't quite know what to think of you, Whitney.'

'The challenge is to keep it that way, right? How about dinner tonight, to make up for the one I had to cancel?'

'Sorry. Tonight the boyfriend isn't working. You know how it is.'

Not any more I don't, Whitney thought. 'Some other time, then.' She felt just a little lonely as she went back to her office. Max had said something about taking her to dinner tonight; it was her first night back in town. But he hadn't called.

Well, I'm not waiting around for Max, she decided. I'm not going to let him take me for granted.

As Charles had. She had thought Charles was the most wonderful thing on earth, at first. She had waited for him, tagged after him, worshipped him, and never once recognised the selfishness that lay at the centre of his nature. She had mistaken it for charming nonchalance. After their wedding, when he was no longer pleased by the attention she lavished on him, and started to accuse her of nagging instead, she had believed that their problems were entirely her fault. She had tried so hard to please him. Then, slowly, the worship had turned to fear, and then to self-loathing, and then to nothing at all, just an emotional vacuum, an empty acceptance that things would never change.

She might have left him then, except for the deep-seated conviction that marriage was for life, for better or worse, and that there was no honourable way to retreat from the horrible mistake she had made.

It was time for the store to close. She walked through slowly, alert for last-minute customers who were sometimes hurried or treated rudely even in the best-run stores. The lights dimmed, department by department, the big doors were locked, the security guards with their dogs took over. Whitney left through the employee doors and set out to walk back to the hotel, glad of the exercise.

Indian Summer had come, but the warm afternoon was quickly giving way to cool evening as the sun sank. The trees along the Plaza's streets were brilliantly draped in red, yellow, and gold leaves, like torches against the solid brick and tile. The fountains splashed frantically, as if knowing it would not be long before winter stilled their splendour for another year.

In a crazy way, she thought, it was nice to be back in Kansas City. Here, for the next few weeks, she would have a little time to notice the seasons passing by. How long had it been, she wondered idly, since she had really noticed the colour of a tree in the autumn? Oh, she could see them from her window at home—if she ever took the time really to look.

She had been two days on the road getting back to Kansas City, with her car haphazardly piled with clothes and a few items to make the hotel suite liveable-in. Not that any number of material things could really do the job; the Henry the Eighth's plastic antiquity was quickly becoming a bore, and Whitney wasn't sure if she could take a whole month of living in two tiny rooms. But at least it was two rooms she could call her own.

That was more than she had had with Charles, she reflected. They had lived in comfort, in a large and luxurious apartment. Whitney's money had paid for it, as she had paid for everything. When they had married, she had thought it a bargain—trading her money for Charles's charm, for his love.

But there had been not a corner of the flat that was exclusively hers. There was no place for her to retreat, no private place to sit and think. She had felt disloyal for even wanting such a thing. A bride shouldn't need to escape from her husband, she thought. Whitney had craved privacy, and she had immediately decided that the fearful need meant there must be something wrong with her. She began to try even harder to make herself into the woman she thought she should be. But the more she worked at it, the less she succeeded, and the unhappier she became.

And then she had found out about the other women. There had been a succession of them, and Whitney was hurt and furious to discover that, indirectly, she had paid for them as well. It was hard to swallow the anger, but she had done it eventually, telling herself that if she could only have succeeded in making herself the sort of wife Charles wanted he would never have looked at another woman. Perhaps she had never been meant to be married at all, she thought. Her career had been too important to her, and Charles had been left alone much of the time. No wonder he had looked about for other entertainment. No wonder he got so angry with her.

She had succeeded in making herself believe it, until the day that Ross had seen the faint shadow of bruises under the long sleeve of her dress. Usually she wore dark colours, because they disguised the marks. But that day she was wearing pale blue. It was summer, her rebellious heart had said that morning, and she was tired of dark, drab clothes. Besides, the bruises had faded, and there hadn't been an incident in almost a week. Surely no one would notice.

But eagle-eyed Ross had, and Whitney had been stunned by the venomous things he had said about Charles. She had never dreamed that Ross felt so strongly about her husband. That afternoon she had found herself sitting beside Ross in the quiet office of the most respected woman psychiatrist in Chicago. After the first half-hour, the doctor had eased Ross out and then looked silently across her desk at Whitney, who was shredding one tissue after another.

'I don't understand him,' Whitney had burst out. 'Ross, I mean.'

There was a brief island of quiet in the office. Then the doctor said, in her grandmotherly way, 'Why do you think he brought you here, Mrs Lattimer?'

'He said he thought Charles would kill me some day, if I didn't do something,' Whitney said reluctantly. Another long silence. Then she added, 'But he's my husband! He wouldn't do that!'

'Is that what you really think?' It was a mere breath of a question, calm, not accusing. 'Or do you feel that you're expected to say that?'

Somehow, Whitney thought vaguely, time didn't pass inside this quiet room. The whole universe had silently wound itself down, and inside her she felt a knot begin to loosen. 'I think sometimes he wants to kill me,' she whispered.

It was the first crack in the wall that she had constructed so carefully in the year of their marriage. It took another six months of quiet hours with the doctor to break down her loyalty to Charles, to help her see that he was not what she had pictured him to be, that perhaps the failure of their marriage was not entirely her fault.

Charles had refused to see the doctor. If Whitney wanted help with her problem, he said, that was fine with him. But there was no reason for him to be involved.

And things had stayed much the same. There would be a month of so when it seemed to be getting better, and Whitney would begin to think that the worst was over. Then something would set him off again, and she would despair.

Eventually, she had stopped seeing the doctor. It did no good, and Charles always seemed to be worse after she had had a session.

She buried herself instead in her work. Tyler-Royale was the only place where she felt competent, valuable—able to cope with problems and make a contribution. If it hadn't been for her work, she didn't know what she would have done.

But the more she retreated into Tyler-Royale, the worse Charles became. Eventually, even Whitney reached breaking-point—the moment when she knew that nothing could be worse than the pain she was suffering.

That was when, one morning after a particularly bad night, she had told him coldly that she could stand no more, that she intended to get a divorce. She had not been emotional. She had not yelled or screamed, or begged. There had been no emotion left in her by then, except for pain. And that had been the day——

Stop thinking about it, she told herself fiercely. It does no good to think about it! Think about Ross instead, and how happy he and his wife were, to have their baby son.

It's no good getting sentimental about that, either, she thought. That was fine for Ross and Kelly. They were the lucky ones, and little Andrew was just one more bond between them. For me, she thought, it wouldn't have worked that way. A baby would have been another source of jealousy, nothing more than that. I would have devoted myself to the child, and Charles would have been angrier yet.

Well, there was no sense getting worked up about it, she decided. All of it was long past. The truth is, she told herself, that I wasn't cut out to be married.

There had been a few men who, over the past couple of years, had shown an interest in her. She had dated once in a while, mostly just to keep Ross from accusing her of retreating into a cave. She had played the games, carried on the polite conversations, submitted to the goodnight kisses. But it hadn't meant anything to her. She didn't want to get involved, and the men had been quickly and easily discouraged. It hadn't taken much to send them away, Whitney remembered. One of them had told her, after she politely declined to go to bed with him on their first date, that she was the most frigid woman he had ever met. And he was probably right, Whitney thought. She wasn't like other women. She never had been, even in the early days with Charles.

She found herself staring into the sparkling depths of a fountain, where coins gleamed against the tile of the basin. Not that she had really cared when that man hadn't asked her out again, she thought. It hadn't been Whitney herself that he was interested in. There were a lot of men who liked the idea of being married to the Tyler-Royale department stores. Most men were really just like Charles at heart.

A sudden shout broke into her thoughts. 'Whitney!'

A little black sports car dodged traffic and double-parked illegally near her.

'Max!' she said. He looked wonderful, she thought, with his dark hair wind-ruffled. No, she thought. I can't be breathless because of seeing Max. I've just walked up the hill too fast.

He leaned across the seat and called out the window, 'I tried to catch you at the store. Cindy spotted you there today.'

'I didn't see her. She should have reminded me about her hat.'

'I'll tell her you haven't forgotten it. Get in; I'll take you to the hotel.'

The hill was steeper than she had expected it to be, and her shoes weren't made for walking. Besides, there was no reason for her to be feeling this awkward shyness. That last crazy phone conversation with Max was nothing to be self-conscious about; he had probably forgotten it altogether. So Whitney got in.

'You didn't let me know you were back,' he accused lightly.

'I've been busy.'

'We do have a dinner-date,' he reminded, and turned a blinding smile on her. 'Remember? We arranged it four days ago over breakfast in bed.'

Whitney tried unsuccessfully to fight down the blush. 'You'd better be careful who you say that to,' she warned.

'Why? It's perfectly true. I only wish we'd been having breakfast in the same bed.' He nudged the car into a spot that was scarcely large enough for it, and said, 'I haven't had a decent night's sleep since, if you want to know the truth.'

'Surely you aren't blaming me for that?' He certainly didn't look as if he was staying up nights, she thought. His eyes were bright, and he looked perfectly well rested. His sports coat was a well chosen tweed, and today he was actually wearing a tie.

'Of course I'm blaming you. It wasn't my fault you weren't here.' But his smile was carefree. 'I suppose you want to change clothes before dinner?'

"I really didn't take you seriously, Max.'

'You'd better start.'

There was a note in his voice that brooked no argument. It made her all quivery inside. Surely he should have got the message by now that she simply wasn't interested? Any other man would have given up long ago. But Max—Max was like a mediaeval knight, she thought, laying siege to a castle and too stubborn to admit that the fortress would never surrender.

He guided her into the hotel gift-shop and fished in his pocket for enough change to buy the evening paper.

'Something to keep me occupied while I wait,' he said blandly.

'Max, you really don't need to come up with me.'

'After what happened last time? I plan to sit in the living-room and yodel just to keep you awake.'

'Last time I had jet-lag, Max——' She gave up. There was no way to win an argument with the man. The only dignified thing to do was to refuse to quarrel.

The gleam in his eyes said that he knew quite well what she was thinking, but he didn't say a word.

At the door of the suite, Whitney paused in irritation. 'Damn,' she said. 'I forgot to pick up a key. When I checked in, I left the car for the bellboy to unpack, and I didn't even come upstairs.'

Max, looking innocent, reached into his pocket. 'Would this do you any good?' he asked.

She looked at the big brass key he was holding. 'You said you were going to turn that back in,' she reminded.

'Yes, I did,' he agreed cheerfully. 'But I didn't say when.' He unlocked the door and ushered her across the threshold with a bow.

'You could just give me the key.'

He considered it, and shook his head. 'No thanks.' Then he settled himself comfortably on the couch and unfolded the newspaper. 'Guess what. They've developed a new diet to fight jet-lag.'

'Terrific. Where was it when I needed it?'

'I'll order a copy of it for you. By the way, I've got tickets to the Candlelight Ball this weekend.'

'Congratulations. Have a good time.'

'I knew that you'd want to go.'

'Why should I? What's so special about the Candlelight Ball?'

'It's a very big social event, and for public relations value, you really should be seen there.'

'I don't even know what it's all about, Max.'

'That's why I'm taking you. To keep you from putting your foot in your mouth.'

She stood there for a moment and looked down at him. It was well past time to disillusion Max. He seemed to have the idea that she was going to be spending all her spare time with him. Why, she had no idea; there were certainly women who were more willing than she, and more attracted to Max. But convincing him would be something like persuading a steam roller.

'Why are you standing around here?' he asked finally. 'Do you want me to help you undress?'

She blushed beet-red and retreated without a word to the bedroom. It took less than ten minutes to trade her light suit for a long-sleeved dress in a blue that was just the same shade as her eyes. She combed her hair out into a loose black cloud and touched up her make-up, wondering irritably why she was even bothering. There would be no one to impress except Max, and why should she care what he thought?

When she came back to the living-room, he had pushed the newspaper aside and was leaning against the small bar that divided the living-room area from the kitchenette. He looked up when she opened the door.

He didn't say a word, but his eyes widened just a little.

Well, Whitney thought, it was comforting to know that he wouldn't be embarrassed to be seen with her. She reached for her handbag and checked to be sure that her make-up kit was inside. 'Shall we go?'

Max shook his head. 'Not quite yet,' he said. 'There's something I want to do first—something I've wanted to do since I caught sight of you on the pavement this afternoon.' There was a catch in his voice.

She started to ask what it was, but before she could get the words out, his arms were around her. Automatically she stiffened, and then forced herself not to panic. It was only a kiss, after all. In a way, it was almost pleasant that she craved physical contact with another human. When he kissed her again, she almost automatically responded, her lips softening under his, her hand fluttering up to brush the soft hair at his temples

HARLEQUIN

 PRESENTS

A
Real Sweetheart
of a Deal!

PEEL BACK
THIS CARD
AND SEE
WHAT YOU
CAN GET!
THEN...

Complete the Hand Inside ➤

*It's easy! To play your cards right,
just match this card with the cards
inside.*

Turn over for more details . . .

Incredible isn't it? Deal yourself in <u>right now</u> and get 6 fabulous gifts. ABSOLUTELY FREE.

1. 4 BRAND-NEW HARLEQUIN PRESENTS® NOVELS—FREE!
Sit back and enjoy the excitement, romance and thrills of four fan
tastic novels. You'll receive them as part of this winning streak!

2. A PRACTICAL LUCITE CLOCK/CALENDAR—FREE!
You'll love your new LCD digital
quartz clock, which also shows the
current month and date. This lovely
lucite piece includes a handy month-
at-a-glance calendar, or you can display your favorite photo in the calendar area. This is our special gift
free to you with this offer.

3. AN EXCITING MYSTERY BONUS—FREE!
And your luck still holds! You'll also receive a special mystery bonu
You'll be thrilled with this surprise gift. It will be the source of man
compliments as well as a useful and attractive addition to your home

PLUS

**THERE'S MORE. THE DECK IS STACKED IN YOUR FAVOR. HER
ARE THREE MORE WINNING POINTS. YOU'LL ALSO RECEIVE:**

4. MONEY-SAVING HOME DELIVERY
Imagine how you'll enjoy having the chance to preview the romanti
adventures of our Harlequin heroines in the convenience of you
own home at less than cover prices! Here's how it works. Every mont
we'll deliver 8 new Harlequin Presents® novels right to your doo
There's no obligation to buy, and if you decide to keep them, they'
be yours for only $1.99* each! That's 26 cents less than the cove
price and there's <u>no</u> extra charge for shipping and handling!

5. A MONTHLY NEWSLETTER—FREE!
It's "Heart to Heart"—our members' privileged look at upcomir
books and profiles of our most popular authors.

6. MORE GIFTS FROM TIME TO TIME—FREE!
It's easy to see why you have the winning hand. In addition to all th
other special deals available only to our home subscribers, when yc
join the Harlequin Reader Service®, you can look forward to add
tional free gifts throughout the year.

SO DEAL YOURSELF IN—YOU CAN'T HELP BUT WIN

*Terms and Prices subject to change.

You'll Fall In Love With This Sweetheart Deal From Harlequin!

HARLEQUIN READER SERVICE
FREE OFFER CARD

PLACE YOUR WINNING CARD HERE!

4 FREE BOOKS • FREE LUCITE CLOCK/CALENDAR • FREE MYSTERY BONUS • FREE INSIDER'S NEWSLETTER • FREE HOME DELIVERY • MORE SURPRISE GIFTS

Yes! Deal me in. Please send me four free Harlequin Presents® novels, the lucite clock/calendar and my free mystery bonus as explained on the opposite page. If I'm not fully satisfied I can cancel at any time but if I choose to continue in the Reader Service I'll pay the low members-only price each month.

108 CIH CANY

First Name	Last Name
PLEASE PRINT	

Address		Apt.

City	State

Zip Code

Offer limited to one per household and not valid to current Harlequin Presents® subscribers. Orders subject to approval. Terms and Prices subject to change.

HARLEQUIN® NO RISK GUARANTEE
- There is no obligation to buy—the free books and gifts remain yours to keep.
- You'll receive books before they're available in stores.
- You may end your subscription at any time—by marking "cancel" on your statement and returning your shipment of books at our cost.

PRINTED IN U.S.A.

Remember! To win this hand, all you have to do is place your sticker inside and DETACH AND MAIL THE CARD BELOW. You'll get four free books, a free clock/calendar and an exciting mystery bonus!

BUT DON'T DELAY! MAIL US YOUR LUCKY CARD TODAY!

and then to rest at the back of his neck, holding him gently.

'I've missed you, Whitney,' he murmured against her lips. 'I've spent the last four days thinking about you. I want you so much.'

Sanity returned with a jerk. 'No!' she cried. 'I can't, I can't!' Horror swept over her along with the realisation of the position she had put herself in. She tried to push herself away from him.

Max's arms tightened. 'And why not?' he said fiercely. 'Just why can't you kiss me, or make love with me if you want? You're not a child, Whitney.'

'Don't ask me to explain,' she whispered. 'It's not your fault. It's nothing personal, Max.'

'I'm damn well taking it personally,' he growled. He released her abruptly, and Whitney grabbed for the corner of the bar for support. 'One minute you're warm and seductive, and the next——' He paced the room once, and came back to stand in front of her. 'I don't understand, Whitney!'

'Don't hit me,' she whimpered.

'My God, you know how to kick a man when he's down. Hit you? I could no more hurt you than I could take a razor blade to my own——'

He stopped abruptly. For a full minute there was silence in the room, broken only by Whitney's shuddering breaths.

Max rubbed his knuckles against his chin. With a swift economy of motion, he went to the kitchen sink and drew a glass of water. 'Drink this,' he said, and put it in Whitney's hand.

She took a couple of swallows. 'I'm sorry,' she said. 'About thinking you might—hit me. It was automatic.'

Max nodded. 'Yes, I'd noticed that. It wasn't the first time you've flinched away from me, either.'

Whitney shifted the glass from one hand to the other, wondering what he expected her to do with it. He took it from her and drained it at a gulp. His eyes were dark,

and there were two deep furrows etched into his forehead.
He pulled out a chair and pointed to it.

'Sit down,' he said.

She did, meekly.

'Whitney, I think it's time you told me all about it.'
His voice was soft, but it allowed no argument. 'From
the beginning.'

CHAPTER SEVEN

SHE sighed, wearily. 'What's the point, Max? Look, if you want to just walk out of here, I'll understand. We're professionals; we can still work together.'

'You might be certain of that. I'm not sure I'm quite that professional.'

She didn't understand that at all. 'Well, I'm sure you have better things to do with your evening than listen to the story of my life.'

'Whitney,' he said, his voice dangerously soft, 'we are going to sit here till I'm satisfied. So if you want anything to eat tonight, you'd better start talking. Or would you rather I asked questions?'

She didn't answer. She didn't even want to look at him; she was staring at her hands folded tightly in her lap.

'All right,' he said. 'I know Ross well enough to be certain that he's not the one who taught you fear. And I don't think you've had a collection of men in your life. So that leaves only Charles.'

She twisted her fingers together.

'He beat you, didn't he?'

'Please, Max—is this necessary?'

'Yes, I think it is. The only thing I know about Charles, you see, is that Ross detested him. I never knew why.' He pulled out a chair opposite her, then seemed to think better of it and paced the room. 'As a matter of fact,' he said with a wry smile, 'I thought that Ross was mildly amusing. He was so protective of you that I doubted he would ever think anyone was good enough to deserve his little sister.'

'That's a joke,' Whitney whispered.

'Of course, since I didn't even know you at the time, I can't say that the situation was a big worry in my life.'

And it's none of your business now, either, Whitney thought. 'I'd much rather not talk about it.'

'Why?' Max pulled his tie off as if it were choking him and tossed it aside. 'Because you're still so blindly in love with Charles that you can't let another man touch you?'

'No.' The denial was quick and breathless.

'Then what is it? If you were miserable with him, why do you go around in this cloud of "don't bother me, I'm in mourning" all the time?'

'It's easier that way.'

'I'll just bet it is,' Max said brutally. 'You don't have to feel anything.'

She was furious. 'You keep misunderstanding me! I only mean that I made a mess of my marriage——'

'Is that why you said you'll never do it again?'

'Yes. There are some people who were never meant to be married. I'm one of them.'

He sat down on the edge of the table, arms folded across his chest. 'Is Charles the one who told you that?' he asked pleasantly.

'No, Max. I can figure a few things out for myself.' She brushed a wisp of hair out of her eyes. 'Look,' she said, determined to make him understand. 'Charles wasn't a perfect husband——'

'I can see that.'

'All right. He was selfish and he had a violent temper and——' her voice cracked '—and there were other women. But it wasn't all his fault. I wasn't woman enough to satisfy him. I nagged at him, and I——'

'Sweetheart,' Max interrupted gently, 'if you weren't enough for him, then that was his problem, not yours.'

It was horribly important, she thought, that she make him understand. 'There is something wrong with me,' she said, brokenly. 'I just can't feel what other women feel.'

Max lifted an eyebrow. 'Is that a roundabout way of telling me that you're frigid?'

She shivered at the very word. 'I suppose so, yes.'

'After living with Charles, it is no wonder. The man was a raving psychotic, Whitney.'

'But that doesn't excuse what I did,' she said, There was a long silence, and then she gathered all her courage and blurted out the words. 'I killed him, Max.'

My God, she thought. I don't believe I said that . . .

There was a long silence. Max's face was suddenly chalk-white beneath his tan. He shook his head a little, as if he was trying to clear it. 'I thought Ross told me that Charles cracked up his car on the expressway.'

Whitney dashed tears out of her eyes. 'He did.'

'Were you in the car?'

'No.'

'Then I don't understand. How did you kill him? Did you hire somebody to tinker with his engine?'

'Of course not.' She wiped her wet cheeks with the back of her hand.

He gave her a handkerchief. 'Then how?'

'I told him I wanted a divorce, that I couldn't bear living as we were.' She blew her nose and blotted her eyes. 'And then I went to work as usual. He came to the store that morning. He wanted me to come with him—we'd talk about it, he said. But I told him I didn't have time to talk to him any more. I was through. I'd made up my mind.'

Max's jaw tightened. He seemed to be gritting his teeth.

'I didn't mean it,' she said. 'I thought perhaps he'd be shocked into doing something about it, if he thought I was really going to leave him.' She folded the handkerchief between her fingers. 'He left,' she went on painfully. 'I expected him to argue, but he didn't. He just left. Two hours later they called me. He'd wrapped his brand-new Porsche around a concrete bridge pillar on the Dan Ryan Expressway.'

'That was just a bit coincidental, don't you think?'

'There was nothing coincidental about it, Max. There were no skid marks. The witnesses said he drove straight into it.'

'The interpretation seems perfectly obvious to me.'

She nodded, and murmured, 'I should have gone with him.'

Max's jaw tightened. 'You must be joking. He'd only have taken you into the bridge with him. He'd probably planned it that way.'

'But don't you see? I sent him away. Perhaps if I'd only tried to talk to him, to explain...' For the first time, she was saying things that had haunted her for three years. It didn't seem to matter that it was Max she was talking to; she hardly knew he was there.

'It wouldn't have made any difference, except that you would have been dead too.'

'Maybe I should have been.' It was only a murmur.

He swore under his breath. 'You can't mean that, Whitney.'

'No, I don't think I do. But I'd taken away his reason to live.' Her eyes, deep pools of tear-drenched blue, pleaded with him for understanding.

'That's exactly right. It sounds to me as if the man got his biggest kicks out of hurting you. You'd told him to get out of your life. He couldn't hurt you in any of the old ways any more, so he found a new one.'

It was the first time she had ever looked at it quite that way. It startled Whitney. Was Max right? she wondered. Could he be right? Of course not, she told herself. Max had never even met Charles.

'He left a note, of course,' Max said.

She was startled. 'How did you know?'

'Charles's kind always do.' His voice was savage. 'What did he say?'

'I don't know.' She sounded ashamed of herself. 'Ross never let me see it.'

'Oh, that was stylish. He addressed it to Ross?'

'Not exactly,' Whitney said reluctantly. 'He posted it that morning, after he left the store, to a reporter at the *Sun-Times*. By the time it was delivered, of course, Charles was dead. Ross and the reporter were friends, so——'

'Good God,' Max's face was grim. 'What was he hoping for, headlines? He wanted to go out in a blaze of glory, I suppose, to show you and the world how important he was. Well, he accomplished his purpose, didn't he?'

'He certainly ended his misery,' Whitney murmured.

'Who gives a damn about him? I was thinking about your misery, instead. He's kept you from living, by making you feel guilty over his death. Which is exactly what he intended.'

She swallowed hard. 'I was a part of it, Max. I was responsible.'

'Oh, really?' He walked across the living-room and slid the glass door back. 'I think I'll go out on the balcony and jump because you won't bleach your hair to please me.'

She followed him. 'Max, that's ridiculous!' A fresh breeze billowed the curtain and made Whitney shiver. Or was it fear, instead? What was Max thinking? She had never seen him look this way, act this way——

A leaf blew through the opening and caught in her hair, and she picked it out with shaking fingers.

'You're right,' he said, leaning against the wrought-iron railing. 'It's ridiculous. You'd look awful as a blonde. But if I'm crazy enough to want to end it all, that's my choice—no matter what excuse I choose to give.'

'Max, you make me scared.'

'But whatever I say can't make it your fault.' He guided her back into the living-room and closed the glass door. 'Fortunately for you, I don't want to jump. I would much rather take you into the bedroom and teach you that frigidity is entirely in the imagination.'

She drew back, horrified.

'Don't worry. I'm not going to do it. But I'd certainly like to.'

She was shivering. 'This is not a joking matter. There are women like that—women like me——' Her heart was slamming against her ribcage with every beat. I have to make him understand, she was thinking.

'Possibly,' Max conceded. 'I haven't surveyed every female in the species. But as for the idea that you're one of those women——' He shook his head, slowly and emphatically.

Whitney turned her back on him. She was trembling as she sat down, and her fingers shook as she carefully, mindlessly, arranged the skirt of her dress into tiny pleats.

Max put a gentle hand on the nape of her neck, under the cloud of hair. His touch was gentle, and the warmth of his hand soothed the tense muscles there.

'I think you'd better tell me everything,' he said.

She closed her eyes and focused her attention on the warm, strong hands massaging her neck and shoulders. Slowly she began to speak, as if she were hypnotised into remembering the months of her marriage. She told him things that she had never confided in anyone else, not even in Ross. Sometimes her voice cracked, and once she had to stop for a few moments to regain her composure, but Max's hands never faltered in their gentle soothing. Finally, she stopped talking.

'That's it?' he said softly. 'You're not still holding something back?'

'You can't want to hear all this,' she protested.

'No. It's pretty filthy. But unless I know it all, I can't be sure that I won't do something awkward and frighten you again. And I do not want to frighten you.'

Whitney thought that over for an instant, and started to cry. 'Do you mean—you aren't disgusted by me?'

He bent over her and put his cheek against her hair. 'Not only am I not disgusted,' he said huskily, 'but I think you're one hell of a girl. You're strong and brave and beautiful——'

She dried her tears. 'It's sweet of you to say that, Max.' She tried to laugh.

'It's also true, dammit. I can't be the first man who's told you these things.' His hands tightened on her shoulders as if he were afraid she would slip away. 'And if your reason for confiding all that was to discourage me, you failed. I still want to make love to you.'

'You're a masochist, Max.' She smiled tremulously up at him. 'Or a lovely liar. At the moment, I don't even care which it is.'

'Don't you?' Abruptly he let go of her.

For an instant Whitney felt cold and abandoned. Then she fought off the sensation. How silly of her to feel that without his warm touch, she was alone in a threatening world! 'You wouldn't find it a very enjoyable experience, I'm sure.'

'Shouldn't I be the judge of that?'

'Why? I can save you the trouble. I've told you, Max——'

'I know. You've tried making love, and you don't like it. Well, that wasn't making love, Whitney. You can call it whatever you like, I suppose, but if it isn't a partnership, then it's only a mechanical act. You didn't trust Charles. You were afraid of him.'

'Why should you bother with me?' she asked lightly. 'There are a million other women——'

'Because if someone doesn't wake you up, you're going to become a neurotic old maid, wallowing in your guilt. All I want to do is prove to you that Charles was the unsatisfactory one. Not you.'

'I see. You're a crusader, trying to stamp out social problems——'

'I didn't exactly ask for the job,' Max pointed out, 'but I'll take it on, because you're too nice a woman to waste your life over a jerk like Charles. Now, wash your face and let's go out to dinner and banish the blues.'

* * *

She was uneasy at first, afraid that Max would pursue the subject over dinner. I shouldn't have come, she told herself when he waved the *maitre d'* aside and held her chair himself—choosing the one beside him rather than the seat across the table. She half expected that he would want to hold her hand, or kiss her, or amuse himself with off-colour banter, or—worse yet—discuss what she had told him about her months with Charles. Just exactly what had she told him, she wondered with a trace of panic. She could remember bits and pieces——

But Max seemed to have forgotten the interlude entirely. He was charmingly casual throughout the meal, and it was only when Whitney was finishing her chocolate torte that he set his coffee-cup down and said, 'Now we need to discuss a few important things.'

Whitney froze, her fork half-way to her mouth.

Max didn't seem to notice. 'The Candelight Ball, for instance,' he went on. 'I can't drag you there, of course, but it's very important that you go.'

The terrible tight pressure in her chest eased a little. 'Why?' she asked.

'Use your head, Whitney. The social snobs may not be the only sort of people you want to draw into Tyler-Royale, but they're important. And you can only get them if they feel you're up on their level. Therefore, the Candelight Ball is a necessity.'

'Max, I'm only the temporary manager. What difference can it possibly make whether I go to this dance?'

'How long will you be here?'

''A month, perhaps.'

'That's long enough to make a considerable difference in the image of the store.' He looked at her quizzically over the rim of his cup. 'What are you really objecting to? Do you dislike the social bit that much, or are you afraid to go with me?'

Whitney pushed the crumbs of her torte around on her plate, and refused to meet the challenge in his eyes. 'A little of both, I should think,' she admitted finally.

'And why would you be afraid of me, I wonder?' he mused. 'Are you, perhaps, concerned that I might talk you into doing something you would later regret?'

'You couldn't talk me into anything.'

'We won't argue about that. I promise you, however, that you wouldn't regret it. But that's beside the point, because I will not push you into sleeping with me. Just let me know when you're ready.'

Whitney's mouth dropped open. The arrogance of the man was beyond belief, she thought. 'Don't hold your breath,' she warned. 'It's getting late, Max, and we both have work to do tomorrow.'

He smiled at her. 'Are you running, Whitney?' he asked, softly. But he rose and held her chair and said no more.

The pressure of his hand on the small of her back as they left the restaurant was light. It was nothing more than good manners, what any man might have done. But somehow Max turned the casual gesture into an intimate caress.

Whitney was having a little trouble keeping her breathing even. But she knew that if she said anything to him about it, he would merely look innocently astounded, and then he would turn it back against her. So she ignored him as best she could.

He insisted on walking her to her suite, and she was braced for the goodnight kiss that she was certain he would want. He might not even ask, she thought; he might just kiss her without warning, as he had that night at the airport. On the other hand, now that he understood the reasons for her hesitation, he might even beg. Well, in any case, she decided, she would be a sport about it. There was no dignity in fighting him, so she would calmly let him take his kiss, and that would be the end of it. She was determined, however, that he would not come inside the suite tonight, no matter how hard he talked.

But he stopped at the door, unlocked it for her, smiled down into her eyes, flicked a finger across her cheek, and turned towards the lift with a cheerful goodnight. He left her standing in the middle of the hotel hallway, blinking in astonishment.

It shouldn't have come as a surprise, she told herself as she climbed wearily into the big bed. With all the garbage she had told him about herself tonight, it was no wonder that his original attraction had vanished. He hadn't really wanted to kiss her, that was apparent; if he had, he'd have done it, even over her objections. All the talk about taking her to the Candlelight Ball, and about taking her to bed, had been just that—talk. Max couldn't wait to get away from her.

And I'm glad, she told herself. That's one problem out of the way. Now when I get the store settled down, everything will be back to normal.

She went to sleep with her hand against her cheek, the palm cupped over the spot where Max's fingers had so briefly rested.

The security guard was going off duty when Whitney came in through the employees' entrance. He greeted her with a cheerful smile, and even the Dobermann by his side looked happy to see her.

The store had a sleepy, early-morning murmur to it, but here and there were islands of light where departments were coming to life early. From the Terrace Restaurant on the mezzanine floor, the yeasty smell of fresh-baked bread drifted down the escalators.

We'll have to do something about that, Whitney thought. The bread smelled wonderful, until its aroma collided with the perfumed atmosphere around the cosmetics islands.

A half-dozen employees looked up from their work in the separate departments as she passed, and greeted her with unhurried smiles. Whitney remembered nearly every name. Not a bad record, she congratulated herself,

when she considered that she had been the manager of
this store for only three days.

The first morning, she remembered, she had been ignored by the employees on the floor as she walked from
one department to the next. Was it her imagination, or
had there been a turn-around in the mood at Tyler-Royale
already?

Perhaps Max would know, she thought. It was too
early yet for firm results from the surveying, but surely
by now he would have an impression.

Karen Emerson was in the employees' lounge, pinning
a white carnation on the lapel of her jacket. She looked
at Whitney and then up at the clock on the wall.
'Goodness,' she said. 'And to think that I've worked for
promotions all these years in the fond belief that once
I had my own store to manage, I didn't have to come
in at ghastly hours of the morning.'

Whitney reached for a white carnation of her own.
'Sorry, dear. That only works with stores that are running
well.'

'This one is a thousand per cent improved, compared
to a week ago.'

'Do you really think so? I couldn't decide if it was
getting better. It might be only a bunch of employees
who are trying to butter up the boss by showing up early
and smiling.'

Karen chuckled. 'Oh, there's a little of that, no doubt.
There always is. But at least everyone is talking again.'

'Were you serious?' Whitney asked. 'About being interested in store management, I mean.'

Karen shrugged. 'Of course, eventually.'

'It might pay to do something about it now,' Whitney
mused. 'The whole chain is short of top management.
That's why I'm here.'

'I wondered, but I didn't like to ask. I thought perhaps
you'd got tired of the travel and decided to settle down.'

'Me? Settle down?' But Whitney was aware that under
her jeering tone was a tiny mournful cry. I miss having

my own things around me, she thought. I don't miss my friends, exactly, but I miss the idea of something reliable in my life—a pattern to live with.

Heaven knew, she thought, there had been few enough friends while she was married, and fewer who had remained loyal through the long months after Charles died. No, she wouldn't miss those people. But it would be nice to make new friends—to put down roots somewhere. Even her apartment in Chicago was only rented. It wasn't as if it was really hers.

Funny, she thought. That's the first time I've ever thought of it quite that way—as if I'm a plant gasping for earth to feed me. And I'm the one who teased Ross when he bought a house in the suburbs!

Karen was looking at her quizzically. Whitney pulled herself back and said, lightly, 'I've got used to the travel.'

'Does that mean you won't be staying in Kansas City?'

'That's right.'

Karen shook her head. 'I think that's a mistake. We've had enough uproar here without another switch in management.'

'Sorry to disappoint you, but that's the plan.' Whitney glanced at her watch. 'I think you should write Ross a letter about the top management positions.'

'It would mean going back to Chicago for training, wouldn't it?'

'Yes, but it would only be for a few months.'

'Then I'd be transferred,' Karen said thoughtfully. 'And it could be anywhere.'

'Only if you agreed to go. Ross never sends anyone to a store they don't want. Except me, that is,' she added wryly. 'Would your boyfriend object?'

'Probably. I'll have to think about it. He's—well, he's pretty important to me.'

And that, Whitney thought as she went on to her own office, was why Karen Emerson would probably never manage a Tyler-Royale store. It was sad.

Or was it? she asked herself. Karen had a good job now, as a fashion buyer. She managed her department well, and it was one of the few in the Kansas City store that had held firm through the turmoil. And she had a man in her life, too, a man who was obviously very important to her. Perhaps Karen already had everything she really wanted.

Whitney, she told herself, you sound just a little jealous. And that was the most ridiculous thing possible.

Georgia was already at her desk. 'Mr Clayton called a few minutes ago.'

Ross? What could he want, this early in the morning, Whitney wondered. 'Thanks, Georgia. I'll want the customer service files today, by the way. Every complaint letter we've had since the store opened, and the response that was made to it.'

Georgia sighed wearily. 'Yes, Mrs Lattimer.'

Ross called again within minutes. 'It's nothing dreadfully important, Whitney,' he said. 'I just wanted to bring you up to date.'

'Have you found my replacement yet?'

'That's the problem. Higgins and Hunter said no, unconditionally. I can't blame them; they're settled members of their communities, and they've been there for years.'

'I can't believe they refused.'

'Obviously, you were wrong about me. My swinish arrogance, I think you called it,' Ross said, with a note of hurt humility. 'Neither of them showed the least fear of refusing me, and Higgins actually laughed when I asked him. He said they'd removed him from San Francisco in a box and please not to suggest any future improvements in his career unless they were really improvements.'

'Well,' Whitney said, trying to be fair, 'I can't blame him. He does love the beaches and the weather. But that still leaves Loomis.'

'I've asked. He said he'd talk to his wife and get back to me.'

The door of Whitney's office opened, and Max peered around it. She cupped her hand over the telephone. 'Max, Georgia is supposed to announce my visitors.'

'I'm not a visitor; I'm a regular.' He sat down across from her and propped his feet on the edge of her desk. 'Georgia has given up on making me behave as she thinks appropriate.'

'Haven't we all.' Her tone was dry, but she had to admit that she wasn't displeased at seeing him. He had been in and out for the last few days—so much so that once she had asked him irritably if he had no other clients. But he never stayed long, and the conversation had never got close to the intimate level that it had that night in her hotel suite.

At least, she had to admit, it seemed that his interest was strictly Tyler-Royale. He had scarcely touched her in the last few days. A casual gesture once in a while— putting his hand on her arm to make a point, or touching her almost by accident when he reached for a pencil— that was the extent of it.

He hadn't been back to her hotel suite, and he hadn't offered to take her to dinner. And he had said nothing more about the Candlelight Ball. Whitney was glad that she had read his intention early. It would have been very embarrassing to have bought a dress for the occasion, and then discover that Max had changed his mind.

She couldn't help being sad, though. Obviously, she thought, what she had told him about Charles and her marriage had made a very big difference in how he thought of Whitney Lattimer.

You sound as if you're complaining, she told herself. It's much easier this way than it was when he was making passes all the time. You should be glad.

But if it was easier, she wondered, why did it make her so irritable?

'Whitney?' Ross asked. 'Are you still there?'

She dismissed her feelings as the ramblings of an overworked mind. 'Yes, Ross?'

'What do you think of Max by now?'

She looked up, guiltily, at Max. 'Umm—would you like me to put him on and he can tell you all about his findings?'

'I see,' Ross said. 'You don't want to talk about him because he's standing right there. That's all right. Just think it, and I'll read your mind. I was always rather good at that.'

'Do you want to talk to him, or not?'

'No. He called me last night. I'll let you get back to him.'

'No hurry,' Whitney said crisply. Ross laughed and hung up.

'He didn't want to talk to you,' she told Max.

He looked vaguely hurt. 'Nobody loves me any more,' he complained. 'You won't have anything to do with me——'

Whitney cut off that line of talk before it could proceed. Perhaps he wasn't disgusted by her after all, she thought, and smothered the tiny note of gladness just as soon as she recognised it. Instead, she told him about her impression that the store was becoming friendlier.

Max nodded, but there was a gleam in his eyes that said he knew quite well why she had changed the subject. 'We're getting a hint of that from the shoppers, too,' he said. 'But a lack of friendliness isn't all that was wrong with this store.'

'I've been thinking about that. I hate paperwork and forms in triplicate—but I think I'll have to add one. We don't have any idea what customers are asking for and not finding. We can't sell what we don't have in stock.'

'Elementary retailing, rule one. And speaking of good ideas—I've been giving a lot of thought to that exclusive little shop of yours—unusual gifts, personal shopping, all that sort of thing. What did you call it?'

'Heart's Desire.' Whitney said reluctantly. Why, she wondered, did I ever share that dream with him? Because I was too tired to watch what I said, that's why.

'It wouldn't make it, of course. Your costs would be too high, and you couldn't pass it all on to the customer.'

'Do you think I don't know that?' Whitney asked crossly. 'I haven't spent ten years in the retail business without learning a few things, Max.'

Max didn't seem to hear. 'But money isn't the only thing that matters to a business. The personal touch would win the loyalty of a lot of customers.'

She pulled a folder across her desk and opened it. 'Is there a point to this, Max? I have work to do.'

'Certainly. My point is that if you could cut your overhead, Heart's Desire might work. And you could do that by trading your biggest asset—the personal loyalty—for heat, light, and all those other unromantic necessities.'

'Who'd be interested in that kind of a deal?'

'Personally, I'd think Tyler-Royale would.' He looked up. 'There are a couple of departments in this store—I'm not sure which ones yet—which I may recommend be combined or eliminated altogether. It would leave space for a new, inventive little department aimed precisely at your favoured market.'

'Heart's Desire,' Whitney breathed.

Max nodded. 'Think about it. If you want to do it, I can write a report that would convince Ross of anything.' He paused at the door. 'By the way, what colour are you wearing to the Candlelight Ball?'

She blinked. 'I'm not, Max.'

'Not wearing anything? Don't you think it's a little cold for a Lady Godiva act? Though I must admit you'll have everybody's attention——'

'I didn't bring any formal clothes.'

'What kind of excuse is that? There's a whole department downstairs. What you're really trying to say is that you'd like to back out—right?'

Whitney stammered a little.

He smiled. 'Now, I never thought you were a coward,' he said softly.

'I thought you'd changed your mind,' she said, goaded. 'You've been hanging around here for days, but you haven't even——' She stopped abruptly, aware that she had said just a little too much.

'I haven't even—what?' Max asked. 'Kissed you? I wondered if you'd notice.'

'I noticed,' Whitney said tartly. 'It was such an enjoyable change!'

'Liar.' From across the room his eyes were warmly caressing. 'I could take care of the omission right now, if you'd feel better.'

'Just go away!'

'Don't you want to be kissed?'

'No.'

'I don't believe you. But you can call me whenever you change your mind.'

'Get out, Max. I have work to do.'

'And I'm distracting you? I'm so glad. But I'm not leaving until you tell me what colour you're wearing to the ball.'

'Blue!' she snapped.

'Periwinkle? Teal? Robin's egg? Turquoise?'

'Why do you care?'

'How about true blue?' he suggested, and was gone before she could reach for something to throw at him.

She was still glaring at the door when Georgia brought the complaint letters in.

So she had misjudged Max again, she thought. He was setting traps for her, and she kept falling into them.

At least there was one thing certain about Max Townsend, she told herself. Nobody could predict what he might do next.

And at least he wasn't ignoring her any more. Foolish, she told herself, to let it matter. What difference could Max possibly make to her?

CHAPTER EIGHT

THERE was a mountain of complaint files. Whitney decided by the time she had waded through the first stack, dictating answers where she could, that filing was apparently all the attention the complaints had ever got.

'Didn't anyone around here ever write to these people?' she asked in desperation in mid-afternoon.

Georgia looked startled. 'Of course,' she said. 'But so many of the problems needed investigation, and then by the time we got the facts, Mr Ward was busy with other things——'

'And so the letters were never answered,' Whitney sighed. 'Write a form letter, Georgia—something about how we regret that your problem was overlooked and that we will now be checking into the matter and getting back to you. Send it out to every one of these people.'

Georgia looked at the stacks of letters, and said, sounding bemused, 'All of them?'

Whitney nodded. 'Except for the ones we've already handled. And from now on, every letter—no matter what it's about—will be answered by return mail. If we can't give a complete answer right away, then we'll just thank the person for writing, but a partial, prompt response is better than having to wait for a full one.'

Georgia was learning not to argue. 'Yes, Mrs Lattimer,' she said, sounding resigned.

Whitney smiled. 'I know, Georgia,' she said. 'I'm not looking forward to this any more than you are. But it has to be done.'

Georgia picked up the fat folders. 'I forgot to tell you,' she said. 'The manager of the confectionery department brought up a parcel for you this afternoon. I don't know

what's in it, but it smells awful.' There was a question
in her voice.

Whitney laughed. 'Two pounds of horehound drops,'
she said. 'Well, that didn't take long. See that they're
sent out to Emma Meadows, will you? I have her address here somewhere.' She flipped through the address
file on her blotter.

'Gladly,' Georgia said. Whitney had never heard so
much enthusiasm in the woman's voice.

'On second thoughts—don't bother. I'll take them out
to her.' I've been putting in long days, she thought. And
this is public relations for the store, too. It's probably
more important than Max's precious Candlelight Ball.

Max, she thought. Why was it that she couldn't just
banish the man from her mind?

'I'll bring the packet right in,' Georgia volunteered.

'It smells that bad?'

The secretary shivered artistically.

'In that case, I'll rescue you from it right now,'
Whitney reached for her handbag and the jacket of her
wool suit. 'I'll see you tomorrow, Georgia.'

'I don't know how many of these letters will be ready.'

Whitney shrugged. 'It took six months to get into this
dreadful shape. I expect it will take a week or two to get
out of it.' Hopefully, she thought, by the time the new
manager takes over, he can start with a clean slate. It
doesn't seem quite fair, though, that I'm doing all the
work and won't ever get to enjoy the results.

But she smothered the twinge of disloyalty. That was
her job, after all. The troubleshooter never got to stay
around and bask in the glow of achievement. There was
always another problem to be solved.

As she took the escalator down to the second floor,
the brilliant colours of the racks of dresses caught her
eye, and she stopped to check out the formal-wear department. She glanced idly at the rack holding her size,
wishing that she had the nerve just to ignore Max.

Perhaps, if she told him that she couldn't find a thing that she wanted to wear——

Max wouldn't buy it, she thought. With all Tyler-Royale to choose from, there had to be something that she could appear in. She might as well give in with a good grace.

Karen Emerson waved at her from the sportswear section, and Whitney called, 'How formal is the Candlelight Ball?'

Karen shifted a rack of clothes and walked across the display floor. 'Very. I saw a gold lamé gown go out of here yesterday.'

Whitney sighed. 'I was hoping to get by with something simple.'

'Oh, you can, as long as it's elegant. Very elegant.' Karen ran a practised eye over the rack, and stopped at a plain white chiffon dress with a pearl-beaded bodice. 'How about this? It's simple.'

'Don't you think it might be a little too bridal?' Whitney asked dryly.

'You could always add red gloves and shoes, and a bright scarlet feather in your hat——' Karen giggled.

'That kind of attention I do not need.' Whitney reached for a bit of royal blue that was peeking out from between two other gowns. 'Something needs to be done about this display,' she murmured. 'It's too crowded.'

'Start by putting about half of the merchandise on clearance,' Karen recommended. 'Normally, I'm very careful what I say about the other buyers, but this batch was a mistake in the first place. Hey, that's pretty.'

The bit of royal blue fabric that Whitney had tugged into view turned out to be the sleeve of a plainly styled dress that dropped straight from shoulder to hem, uninterrupted by decoration. It would have been far too severe to be pretty, except that every inch of the fabric was covered with sequins.

'It will catch the lights,' Karen said. 'And it will make you look about nine feet tall. You'll be the centre of attention, that's sure.'

'Why I should want to be is beyond me.' Whitney said, and pushed the dress back on to the rack. 'At any rate, I have an errand to run at the moment.'

'Aren't you even going to try it on?' Karen called after her.

From half-way across the store, Whitney shook her head. Karen sighed. 'You don't even know what's good for you,' she murmured.

Emma Meadows lived in a walk-up apartment in a brownstone building in the old section of Kansas City, just blocks from Country Club Plaza. The building was well kept, but its age was apparent.

'Not your average high-rent district,' Whitney murmured, parking her car by the kerb. 'But still nice, for all that.' The street was wide, there were trees along the sides, and the buildings had handkerchief-sized lawns in front. The one in which Emma Meadows lived had planters lining the front steps. In them, red geraniums bloomed bravely, daring the autumn frosts to nip their beauty short.

Miss Meadows lived on the third floor. 'No wonder she takes the bus instead of walking over to the Plaza,' Whitney muttered as she reached the landing. 'Just going down for the post is a major cardiovascular exercise!'

The bell sounded loudly, but at first there was no response. Now what do I do, Whitney thought. I can't leave the silly parcel in the hall, and it won't fit in her letter-box. If I bring it back to the office, Georgia will resign——

Just then the door opened a bare crack. One watery blue eye, surrounded by wrinkles, appeared in the slit. 'Yes?' the quavery voice said suspiciously.

Whitney held out her business card. 'I've brought you something, Miss Meadows,' she said. 'A gift from Tyler-Royale.'

'Oh?' Emma Meadows looked at the card, and then up at Whitney. The eye was no less suspicious.

'We've had a new deliver of horehound drops,' Whitney said. 'I brought you a few, because I know how much you missed them.'

The door opened a quarter-inch further. Miss Meadows eyed the packet in Whitney's hand, and then looked straight at her. 'There's more than a few there.'

'A couple of pounds,' Whitney admitted. 'We are very sorry that the mistake occurred, and we hope that you'll accept this as an apology.'

There was a brief silence, as if Emma Meadows was struggling with herself. My gosh, Whitney thought, the woman is going to cry!

The door opened a little further. Emma Meadows' lower lip was quivering, and two tears had slid down the furrows that channelled her cheeks. 'Pardon me for keeping you standing here, Mrs Lattimer,' she said, with dignity. 'Won't you come in and sit?'

'I'd like that.' Whitney handed over the packet, glad to be rid of it, and followed Emma Meadows into the tiny sitting-room.

She was undeniably curious about her hostess. The man in the confectionery department had predicted one thing correctly; Miss Meadows was wearing black. But to Whitney, the old-fashioned dress looked scrupulously clean, as did the crowded, overheated little room they were sitting in. A tabby cat stalked into the room and eyed Whitney.

Miss Meadows said, 'Would you have tea with me? I can make it in a minute.'

'Oh, I wouldn't want to put you to any trouble.' Whitney saw the woman's face fall. Why, she's lonely, she thought. It isn't the tea she cares about, it's someone to talk to. 'But I'd love to stay for tea, if you're sure it's no bother.'

Miss Meadows bustled out, and Whitney leaned back in her chair and looked around. The sitting-room was small and cramped, and every flat surface was covered with knicknacks. A couple of old photographs in carved frames occupied a place of honour on the mantel. It was apparent that the fireplace was no longer used, and a small settee was placed in front of it. The furniture was old and obviously worn, but delicate crocheted lace mats attempted to cover the worst of the threadbare spots. The paper on the walls was old and had started to fade here and there.

Emma Meadows returned with a china plate that held three macaroons. 'The kettle will soon be boiling,' she said. She looked doubtfully down at the plate. 'I haven't much to offer you that's right for tea,' she added. 'I don't have company much, you see.'

The ingenuous admission touched Whitney's heart.

'Such wonderful teas we used to have,' the old lady mused. 'Three kinds of cake sometimes, and scones, too. Mama made wonderful scones, right up to the day she died. Seems like people in Kansas City have all forgotten how we used to have tea,' she said wistfully. Her eyes strayed to the packet, with its distinctive silver Tyler-Royale wrapping paper, on a table near her chair. She looked like a child who had just caught sight of a forbidden treasure.

Whitney gestured towards the packet. 'Please try them,' she said. 'I'd like to be sure they're as good as our regular quality.'

Eagerly, Emma Meadows reached for the box. She picked carefully at the tape, pulling it loose slowly so that the paper wouldn't tear—so slowly that Whitney was ready to scream by the time the box lay open. 'Would you like one?' Miss Meadows asked politely, and it was only when Whitney shook her head that the old lady helped herself.

She sucked thoughtfully, discreetly, at the sweet. 'It's good,' she said, with a contented gleam in her eyes. 'If you'll excuse me, I'll go and make the tea now. The kettle should be boiling.

She returned with the teapot and a single china cup that looked as if it had been hand-painted by an amateur, and filled it for Whitney. 'Aren't you going to have any tea?' Whitney asked.

Mrs Meadows shook her head. 'Oh, no,' she said firmly. 'I'm enjoying my drop just now.'

Whitney was suddenly and uneasily aware that a woman who bought sweets a few pieces at a time might have to watch her budget in other ways as well. She hoped that she wasn't drinking Miss Meadows' entire supply of tea. But it was too late to refuse the cup she held, and too impolite to ask about it. I'll send her some, she thought. We've got some excellent brands at the store.

'It was only a little town,' Miss Meadows said suddenly. The cat had jumped up into her lap, and she stroked the soft fur as she talked. 'The place where I grew up, I mean. And the best part of it was the general store. I'd go there every week with my father, and the shopkeeper would give me horehound drops. I'd go off to a corner and sit to eat one while he and Father talked. But I always saved the rest. Sometimes I had enough to last the whole week out, till the next time we went to the shop.'

She looked up, a little shamefaced. 'I guess I think about those days a lot now,' she admitted.

'It sounds like a wonderful childhood.'

'It was. But then you don't want to hear all about that.'

Whitney sipped her tea. 'Do you live here alone, Miss Meadows?'

She nodded. 'Mama and my sister used to live with me,' she said, sounding rather sad. 'Mama died three years ago. Hazel went last autumn. Now there's just Sheba and me.' She looked down at the cat, purring contentedly on her lap. 'I miss them especially, now that I'm retired. Nearly forty years I taught in the schools around here.' She looked up. 'Hazel and I were both teachers; it was the only suitable job for a woman, Mama used to say when we were growing up. Now women do anything they like.' She sounded wistful. 'I miss the children, though.'

And do they miss you? Whitney wondered. Or are they glad that Old Maid Meadows is gone? Did they ever realise that you needed love, too?

They chatted for a while about the changes in education and opportunities for women, and when Whitney glanced at her watch, she was startled to find that more than an hour had passed. 'I must go,' she said. 'I've taken up your whole afternoon. Thank you so much for tea.'

'Oh, don't go!' Emma Meadows sounded almost panicky. 'Not yet. There is plenty of hot water——'

She's so bitterly lonely, Whitney thought.

The old lady sighed. 'I am sorry. I'm sure you have things you must do,' she said with dignity. 'A husband waiting for you, no doubt, and children.'

No, Whitney thought, with sudden harsh bitterness. I don't even have a cat.

'I hope you enjoy the horehound drops,' she said, at the door.

That brought a smile. 'Two whole pounds,' Miss Meadows said gleefully. 'Don't worry, though. I'll be in on Wednesday, just as usual, and I'll buy some extra.'

Whitney had to smile at that.

'Unless it rains,' Miss Meadows remembered suddenly. 'I can't come when it rains.'

Whitney started down the stairs, knowing that the old lady was watching sadly.

How awful, she thought as she got into her car. That sweet old lady, and all she wants is someone to talk to now and then. She probably hasn't had a guest in months, even years. Her only entertainment is those silly horehound drops, and her cat.

And at that, Emma Meadows is better off than you are, she told herself as she reached her quiet, empty hotel suite. At least she has her home, and her memories, and that cat; you don't have one single living thing that cares about you, Whitney Lattimer!

She stood in the centre of the little living-room, looked around at the institutional furniture, and wanted to scream.

It isn't fair, she told herself suddenly, angrily. Dammit, it isn't fair! Why should I have to be alone like this?

She put her hand on her temple, trying to fend off the sudden, blinding headache that had struck. She flung herself down across the couch and lay there dry-eyed, looking into her future and seeing only emptiness.

'It isn't fair,' she mumbled into the cushion. 'I want more than this from life!'

She lay there for what seemed hours, hearing the small bustling sounds of a busy hotel hallway just outside the door, hearing the idle hum of the small refrigerator and the heating system inside the suite, and hearing most of all the horrifying silence of aloneness.

I've always been alone like this, she thought painfully. Being in Kansas City, away from the few friends who had stood beside her, only made it feel worse—infinitely worse. Here she knew no one, and no one cared for her—except, perhaps, Max.

Max. His name was like a sudden light in a black midnight. She could go to Max, and at least then she wouldn't have to hear the silence. Max would make her laugh. Max would show her how to push the dark dread away.

She was out of the hotel, weaving her little car through the traffic, before she realised that Max might not be at home. Or, if he was, he might not be alone. 'I should have called,' she said. But she refused to go back to that silent suite now. She would drive past his house. If there was no other car, she would stop. And if Max wasn't there——

She didn't even want to think about how she would spend the evening, if she couldn't find Max. She refused to think of it. Max would be at home, because she needed him. He had said she could call him.

The red-brick house seemed to stand aloof at the end of the long drive. It looked dark and deserted from the street, but as her little car crept closer, she saw light pouring from the back of the house, across the drive. She didn't give herself a chance to reconsider; she hurried up the steps to the wide verandah and pounded on the nearest door. Through the bevelled glass panel she could see the gleam of the lights.

The door opened under her hand. Max raised his eyebrows, but said nothing; the telephone was propped between his shoulder and his ear, and the cord was stretched to its limit across a wide kitchen.

Whitney didn't wait for an invitation; she closed the door behind her and leaned against it, soaking up the warmth of the room as if she had been too long in the cold.

Max finished his call and put the telephone aside. 'You look as if you're being chased by demons,' he said.

She straightened up, trying to maintain her dignity. 'Don't sneer at me, Max.'

He guided her across the room to a comfortable couch and sat down quietly beside her. 'I'm not sneering, Whitney. What's happened?'

You idiot, she told herself. You're a grown woman. Why did you come running to Max? Two tears overflowed, despite her best efforts. She wiped them off her cheeks. 'I just need a good cry,' she said, with dignity.

'So cry. You obviously haven't got even a good start, yet. I'll sit here and mop up the mess.'

The tenderness in his voice was the final straw. She burst into tears, and between sobs she told him about Emma Meadows and the horehound drops and the cat and the sudden knowledge that there would be no more than that in her own future.

He held her until the sobs quieted to an occasional shaky breath, and then to silence.

How peaceful it was in his arms, she thought. She was safe there.

'There is really no reason for this concern, you know,' he said finally. 'You aren't frigid. There is nothing wrong with you, apart from the fact that you've been thoroughly scared. Charles was the one who had the problem.'

Was it possible that Max was right? He seemed so certain, and she wanted so badly to believe him.

But just what made him the expert, she thought? What made him so certain that there was nothing wrong with her? He hadn't been there. He didn't know what he was talking about. It was only that monumental male ego of his that made him so certain.

Why should I take the risk, Whitney wondered. What if he's wrong? I'll be the one who will get hurt again! And he might so easily be wrong. He has no first-hand knowledge, except for the couple of times he's kissed me——

But perhaps he had some reason for thinking as he did, she realised. That night at the airport terminal, she had lost all control in Max's arms. She had never felt quite the same way as she had when Max had kissed her. Was it possible that he was right, that she could feel the things she had never known with Charles?

And how will I ever know, she asked herself, unless I take this chance? I'll be a dry, lonely old woman like Emma Meadows——

Max, she thought, looking up at him. He was precious and decent and warm and gentle, and so dreadfully, eminently sane——

'I want to know, Max,' she whispered, and had the eerie sensation that she had just stepped off a cliff, 'will

you help me?' She raised her head from his shoulder
and looked up at him.

He seemed to read the hesitation and the hunger in
her eyes. His arms tightened, ever so slightly, around
her. Whitney felt as if he was looking into her soul, seeing
the hurt there and the questions worn threadbare with
repetition. And he did not look away in disgust, as she
had feared he might. Max would never hurt her——

The breath had caught in her throat. She could find
no words.

My God, she thought, what have I asked of him? I've
made a fool of myself! Perhaps he was only teasing me,
before, when he said all those things. 'If——' she stammered '—if you want, that is.'

Max smiled wryly. 'I must admit it's the most unusual
proposition I've ever received. And yes, I do want to
make love to you, if that's what you're asking.'

I can back out, she thought, with a sudden breath of
relief. He's giving me the opportunity. All I have to do
is say that I changed my mind.

And if I tell him that, I'll always regret it, she thought.
At least be honest with yourself, Whitney, she ordered.
Right now there is no backing out.

'Shall we consider it an experiment?' he said. 'Just
for tonight—the two of us, together.' His fingertips
gently stroked her cheek. 'As for tomorrow—we'll let
tomorrow take care of itself.'

At least he was being honest about it, she thought.
No phony promises, no assurances for the future. Just
honesty, with no strings attached.

And that was what she wanted, too, she reflected. She
didn't care about tomorrow. She only knew that she did
not want to be alone tonight.

She didn't look up at him. She couldn't, right then.
She nodded, a fast, jerky motion as if she was anxious
to have it over with.

There was a twinge of humour in Max's voice. 'Don't
look at me like a child who's about to be punished,' he

begged. His hand rested gently on her cheek, with a new possessiveness in his touch that was like sandpaper against Whitney's skin.

It's only an experiment, she told herself. Stop acting as if it's any big deal! You've been married——

'Do you trust me, Whitney?' he murmured.

Despite the shakiness in her knees and the empty feeling in the pit of her stomach, Whitney discovered that she did trust him, not only to be gentle with her, but to keep her secrets as well. She knew, so certainly that there was no putting it into words, that if this didn't work, no one would ever hear about it from Max. She nodded.

'That, my dear,' he said, 'is the most frightening thing of all.' He tipped her chin up and studied her face. Whatever he saw there seemed to satisfy him, for he rose and held out a hand to her. It was with a childlike faith that she put her hand in his and allowed him to lead her through the dim house.

His bedroom was at the head of the staircase. It was quiet; so far back from the busy street, not even the echo of traffic noises intruded. She stared at the big bed with foreboding, but before her doubts could frame themselves into words, she turned deliberately into his arms. 'Please, Max,' she said, in a little voice that held a sob.

With a murmur that was almost a groan, he pulled her close, and his mouth came down on hers.

For an instant, panic flared, and every muscle in Whitney's body tightened. One muscle at a time, she fought the fear, and forced herself to relax.

It was interesting, she thought as she willed herself to stay calm, the sensations that a mere kiss could arouse. The tingling in her fingertips, for instance—she twisted them in the hair at the back of Max's neck to still their itching. And the wild flutter of her heart beneath the slow, deliberate stroke of Max's fingers over her breast— that was quite interesting. The silk of her blouse seemed

an unnecessary intrusion, and she was conscious of relief
when the last button was released and the warmth of his
palm caressed her.

The very act of undressing her was a seduction in itself,
each piece of clothing removed with the brush of warm
fingers against her goose-bumpy skin. She writhed in
delight under his hands, and her fingers were uncon-
sciously impatient as she tried to respond in kind. She
fumbled with his shirt, and the fabric ripped with a sharp
little screech when a button refused to cooperate.

Gently, Max put her into the bed. He bent over her,
and as his lips brushed the tender skin between her
breasts, the tension that had been building in her ex-
ploded in a shower of desire. It was a feeling alien to
her, something she had never imagined. She looked up
at him with fear-wide eyes, and he seemed to read her
mind.

'It's all right, Whitney,' he murmured against her
throat. 'Don't be afraid——'

His hands were unhurried, gentle, as he caressed each
millimetre of delicate skin. Within her a storm was
building, a passion so furious that there was no room
left for hesitation, or doubt, or fear.

She pulled him down to her with a soft murmur, un-
willing to be separated from him even by the air that
cooled her love-flushed skin. The part of her brain that
could communicate in words seemed to have short-
circuited, leaving touch as the only way to tell him what
she felt. But touch was all the language they needed
tonight.

She knew, in some detached corner of her mind, that
Max was struggling for self-control, and a sense of awe
swept over her at the idea that she could make him feel
that way.

Can this be happening to me, she wondered, and then,
as their bodies joined in the timeless marvel that was
known as making love, she was no longer able to wonder,
or to think at all, only to know with every cell that Max

was right, and that she had never been so much alive as she was at that moment, in his bed.

She didn't know how much later it was before the world stopped its drunken spinning and settled back into a normal orbit. It could have been mere minutes, or hours. Whitney didn't care. She opened her eyes finally, and stared at Max. Then she tried to raise her hand to smooth his tousled hair, but she couldn't make her muscles work quite right. It ought to bother her, she thought, but somehow nothing could disturb her just then.

Max brushed a strand of hair back from her temple, and said huskily, 'If that is your definition of frigid, my dear, I can't wait to see what happens when you thaw.'

She shook her head. Her tongue was thick, but she managed to say, 'You ought to know that nothing like that ever happened to me before.'

'In that case,' he said, 'I suppose I'll have to convince you that it wasn't just a fluke.' His hand wandered over her breast, teasing the love-swollen skin. 'It will be my pleasure.'

'Will it?' she asked, her voice a self-conscious whisper.

He rolled over on to his back and snuggled her against his side, her head on his shoulder. Her hand rested against his chest, and she could feel the strong beat of his heart, slowing a little now, under her ear. She delighted in the masculine smell of him.

'I don't tease about things like that,' he said. He raised her hand to his lips, kissing each fingertip and then tickling her palm with the tip of his tongue. She shivered with the sheer sensual pleasure of it, and he smiled down at her, folded her fingers inside his, and closed his eyes.

A little later, she whispered, 'Max? Was it really special?'

But there was no answer, except a tiny snore.

When she tried to slip away from him, he frowned a little in his sleep, and his arm tightened around her waist.

Whitney sighed. I think I'm being held prisoner, she thought as she snuggled sleepily closer. But there are worse places to be. He's a very, very special man...

How very wonderful it would be, to be his wife...

CHAPTER NINE

THE unbidden thought brought her abruptly back to icy full consciousness. What an idiotic thing to think! she told herself severely. In the first place, Max had made it plain long ago that he intended never to marry. And he could not have said more clearly, before he had made love to her, that as far as he was concerned, this episode between them was only that—an episode.

And besides, Whitney told herself sternly, she was no longer some sort of foolish child, to think that merely sleeping with a man meant that their futures were linked together. That sort of attitude had gone out long ago.

But Max *was* a very special person. She lay there in the circle of his arm, her eyes narrowed in the dim moonlight that poured through the big windows, and watched him sleep. Yes, a very special person, this man who had taken plenty of chances himself this night. It would have been far easier to leave her there in that puddle of self-imposed isolation. But Max had taken the twin risks of rejection and failure, and had succeeded in showing her that there was a world of feeling and desire and sensation buried deep inside her that went beyond anything she had ever imagined.

If she never saw him again, she thought, she would be forever grateful to him for that.

And why on earth, she asked herself crossly, if she was to be humbly grateful for what had happened this night, should she suddenly feel like crying?

Slowly, carefully, she extricated herself from his embrace, feeling a sudden need to be alone. It wasn't easily done; even sound asleep, Max was tenacious. But eventually she was free, shivering in the autumn-cool air. She picked up his shirt and wrapped herself in it and padded barefoot down the stairs.

For the first time she realised that the house was almost empty of furniture. The front parlour, with its window-seat looking out over the veranda towards the street, was furnished only with a plush carpet. The small sitting-room was more comfortable, with deep chairs and books scattered everywhere; obviously it was here that Max spent most of his time. But only the kitchen and his bedroom had been fully furnished. It was as if he had started work on the house and given up, exhausted, in mid-project.

Or perhaps, she thought, he had realised belatedly that the house was far too big for one person, and so he had only furnished the rooms he needed. In any case, it was none of her business. It certainly met Max's standards, and he didn't care what anyone else thought. Max would always make his own rules.

The kitchen was well organised and neat. It didn't surprise her to find that Max ran his house with the same scientific principles he applied in his research. She found the coffee-making supplies all grouped neatly in the cabinet right above the pot, and she filled the glass carafe and started the pot brewing, not because she really wanted coffee but because she needed something to do with her hands.

The cuffs of Max's shirt got in her way, and she paused to roll up the long sleeves. There was a hint of his aftershave in the collar. She rubbed her nose against it, and then—catching herself in the silly gesture—flushed red. How silly, she thought. Just because it was his shirt, she found herself thinking that the touch of the starched fabric brushing against her sensitive skin was like the caress of his hands.

This, she warned herself, is dangerous thinking. She poured the first cup of coffee from the pot and stood sipping it idly, her hands wrapped around the mug.

He was a charming scoundrel. But unlike Charles, Max
didn't demand. Instead, he gave—his patience, his
kindness, his gentle concern. But she was afraid that he
was no less dangerous.

How easy it would be to fall in love with him, she
thought. And what a risk Max had taken—the risk that
she would blindly do exactly that, merely because he was
the first man who had been kind to her. She had almost
forgotten what it was like, to be treated gently, and it
would be so horribly easy to mistake gratitude for a
deeper feeling.

At least she had recognised the possibility, she congratulated herself. How embarrassing it would have been,
otherwise, for her—and how horrifying for Max, who
had only wanted to do her a good turn.

She looked up, sensing his presence. It had not been
any noise that he had made which had attracted her attention, just a sudden awareness that he was there. He
had paused in the doorway, yawning. He was wearing a
brown terry bathrobe, belted loosely, that left most of
his chest bare. She wanted to walk across the room and
put her head down on that warm, solid shoulder.

'You're drinking coffee?' he said. 'It's one o'clock in
the morning.'

'I know it's a switch. Usually you're the one who's
up at odd hours.'

'I'm only up because I found you gone,' he said softly.

She didn't want to explain why she had left his bed.
'I just had a sudden craving for coffee,' she said, with
a shrug. 'I hope you don't mind me helping myself.'

'Mind? As a matter of fact, it looks good. I just draw
the line at women who want to rearrange my furniture.'

Without thinking, she said, 'What furniture?' Then
she could have bitten her tongue. She sounded exactly
like the scheming woman she didn't want to be—the one
who assumed, because he had made love to her, that she
was welcome to take over his life. The kind he had just
warned her not to become.

'I like the airy look,' he complained. 'My mother calls the place a relic and refuses to set foot in it again until I hire a decorator.'

Whitney breathed a sigh of relief. At least he didn't seem to hold the thoughtless remark against her, and for that she was grateful.

Max put his hands in the pockets of the robe, and watched as she reached for another mug. The shirt she was wearing left most of the length of her legs bare as it was, but when she was stretching to reach the cupboard shelf——

'I always did like that shirt,' Max mused. 'But I never before realised the possibilities it held.'

'Oh.' Whitney looked down guiltily. 'I didn't think you'd mind if I wore it.'

'I don't. You may appropriate my whole wardrobe, if you like, as long as you promise to wear it only when I'm around to see.'

For a moment, she wasn't sure if he was being sarcastic, and she stood uncertainly with the brimming mug in her hand. He came across the room to take it from her. But instead of drinking the coffee, he set it aside, tipped her face up, and kissed her lightly on the lips. 'What's wrong, Whitney?'

She wouldn't look at him. 'I just had some things to think about.'

'I was afraid that you might have gone,' he said.

Go back to that lonely hotel suite, in the middle of the night? Or did he really mean that he had hoped to find her gone—out of the way? 'Perhaps I should——'

'You don't really want to go, do you?'

She shook her head. 'No.' It was only a whisper.

'Then you shouldn't go.' There was a brief pause. 'I was an insensitive slob to go to sleep.' He sounded rueful. 'I'm sorry, Whitney——'

She looked up in astonishment. 'Oh, no! It wasn't that, Max!'

He watched her carefully. 'Are you having regrets?'

'No. How could I regret the most beautiful thing that ever happened——' She couldn't finish, because he was kissing her.

This is dangerous, she thought. I should stop this.

Max's mouth demanded her response, and Whitney gasped at the sudden flood of desire that turned her knees to jelly and made her sag weakly in his arms.

Why should I fight it? she asked herself. We're both adults, and we know what we're doing. This isn't going to harm anyone, and if it gives us pleasure—it's only for tonight. Why shouldn't we enjoy tonight?

Max's hands were warm against her quivering muscles, under the shirt.

It did give so much pleasure... Besides, Whitney thought, I still have a lot to learn. And Max is a master teacher...

Then, for a long time, she was incapable of thought. When Max murmured something about getting her warm before she caught pneumonia, she only smiled tremulously, and went with him gladly down the long hall and up the stairs, and back to his bed.

The morning brought reality. She woke alone in the big bed, uneasily aware of the empty pillow beside her. It was early yet, she thought, the sky still grey with dawn, but already Max had left her. The magic had dissipated, she thought. One night, he had said. Just the two of us, for tonight... And now that the night was gone, what came next?

I'm not used to this, she thought, with a twinge of grim humour. I don't know what the proper etiquette is, the correct way to behave on the morning after the night of love——

She pushed the blankets back and went to take a shower. The hard spray stung her skin, but she welcomed the prickly darts. I never noticed before, she thought, that warm water can be a sensual experience!

It seemed that Max had taught her even more than she had thought.

She hesitated a second, and then borrowed his toothbrush. It's obvious that I'm a novice at this, she thought, or I'd have brought my own. But with any luck at all, he'd never know she had used it. She went back to the bedroom, wrapping herself in a big towel. I wonder how long I can put off going downstairs, she thought. Maybe he'll already have left, and I won't have to meet him in the daylight, and wonder if he's thinking about last night, too——

And if I dawdle, she realised, the girls coming to work will have seen my car in the driveway! That's all I need. Whitney reached for the hairbrush on Max's dresser.

It was cool enough for the central heating to have come on, and a gentle stream of warm air brushed over her bare ankles. It reminded her of the gentle touch of Max's fingers across her soft skin, and she shivered under the sudden memories of the sensual pleasures of the night. It was an odd combination of loneliness and gratitude that she was feeling this morning, and it puzzled her a little.

Max walked in while she was attacking the tangles in her hair, and stood in the doorway watching for a moment before she realised he was there.

She met his eyes in the mirror. 'I—I didn't think you'd mind if I used your brush,' she said hesitantly.

He didn't answer. She thought for a moment that he hadn't heard. Only then did she realise that he was carrying a small tray, with two cups on it. He set it aside, carefully, on the trunk at the foot of the bed. Then he came across to her, slowly.

'Max?' she said. 'I'm sorry about the brush——' She didn't know what else it could be that had put him in this odd mood. Some people were touchy about their personal possessions, but she had never thought of Max being that way——

He took the brush from her hand and put his arms around her waist, pulling her back against his chest. The stubble of his beard scratched her temple. 'Whitney, about last night——'

She tensed. He sounded so serious, she thought—she knew what he was going to say. He would warn her not to dream of the future—but Whitney needed no warnings.

'Don't, Max,' she said softly. 'We said there were no strings attached, no expectations.' Then she held her breath. She felt somehow as if she were fighting for her life. She couldn't have explained it, but she knew deep in her heart that talking about last night would make it seem as if it had never happened at all.

He didn't say anything at all for a long moment.

'Please, Max, let's just leave it at that, and enjoy the little time we have.' I want him to know that I'm grateful for what we've already shared, she thought. I don't want him to think that I expect anything at all——

'How long will you be here?' Max asked quietly.

She shrugged. 'A couple of weeks, perhaps. A month at the most.'

He sighed, and her breath seemed to lock in her throat in sudden fear. Will he tell me that he doesn't have two weeks to spend with me, she wondered?

Then he pulled her closer against his chest. 'Do you have any idea how beautiful you are this morning?' His voice was husky. 'And how incredibly sexy, wearing that towel?'

She put her head back against his shoulder. Hot tears of relief stung her eyes, and she closed them to keep him from seeing. 'No,' she whispered.

He turned her gently around in the circle of his arms, and smiled. Whitney's heart turned over. 'Then I'll just have to show you, won't I?' he said.

The towel dropped unheeded to the floor, and the coffee grew stone-cold in the untouched cups.

* * *

'This is utterly ridiculous,' Max said. He said it loud
enough for Whitney to hear him clearly, through the
closed door that separated bedroom from living-room
in her hotel suite.

'What is ridiculous?' she asked mildly. Not quite
enough eye-shadow, she decided, and added another
shade.

'I've seen you getting dressed before, you know,' he
said. 'I don't see why you've banished me
tonight——'

'Because it's a party.' She brushed just a bit more
mascara on to the tips of her lashes. 'And because you
distract me. And because it isn't good for you to see all
the gyrations I have to go through to be beautiful.' There
was a dissatisfied snort from the living-room. 'That gives
you three good reasons to choose from,' Whitney went
on serenely. 'Take your pick.'

'Do I really distract you?'

She smiled, secretly, to herself. Typically male, she
thought, to have gone straight to the only reason that
involved him! She shivered happily at the mere memory
of how he could walk up behind her, kiss the nape of
her neck, and make her forget things like getting to work
on time. But it wasn't good for Max to be told that, so
she said merely, 'Now and then. And we're going to be
late as it is, so I'd rather not be distracted tonight.'

'Damn the Candlelight Ball,' Max said.

'That wasn't what you said about it last week. You
said it was very important for the store that I go.'

'Can I come in so we don't have to shout about it?'

'No.'

'I promise not to touch you.'

'I don't believe you.' In any case, she thought, he
didn't have to touch her to make her go all shivers. He
could do it with a look.

She put the mascara into her small evening-bag and
made a last experimental turn in front of the mirror.
The royal blue sequined gown caught the dressing-lights

and shattered the rays into a million jewels of colour. Not bad, Whitney thought. Not bad at all.

She picked up her velvet cape and opened the bedroom door just as Max said, 'This is cruel and inhuman punishment. I hope you realise——'

He stopped dead as he glimpsed her. 'Oh!' he said, on a note of wonder.

She held out her cape, and he took it absent-mindedly but made no effort to help her into it. 'Now I know why you wouldn't let me in,' he said.

'Do you like it?' Her tone was innocent. His eyes had said all there was to say.

Max tugged at his black bow-tie, as if it had suddenly become too tight. 'You do realise that dress is damned near indecent?'

Whitney raised one eyebrow. 'What makes you say that? It's long-sleeved and high-necked——'

'You must be joking! I said it's indecent because it looks as if you're not wearing anything under it.'

'Oh. That's simple enough to explain. I'm not.'

Max choked a little. 'Nothing?'

'Well, not much.' Whitney smiled. 'Shall we just leave it at that? You look marvellous tonight, by the way.' The severe black of evening clothes was very flattering to him, and the pleated white shirt with the pearly fastenings was a gorgeous contrast to his tanned face.

At the moment, his face looked disgruntled, but Whitney paid no attention. 'My cape, Max,' she reminded him gently. 'We're going to be late.'

He slipped it over the gown. 'We wouldn't be late if you hadn't insisted on coming to the hotel to dress,' he pointed out. 'It was a waste of time.'

'You'd have been objecting about the dress.'

'Ah! So you do think it's a little less than decent!'

'I didn't say that. I just knew what you'd think of it, that's all.'

'You could have got dressed at the house just as well as here,' he said stubbornly.

Reasoning with him was a futile exercise, she had found. Instead of arguing, she said, "Max, I do have an image to maintain.'

'The hell with the image. It would be much easier for both of us if we didn't have to dash back and forth.'

'Would you really want to explain to Ross why I've suddenly moved in with you?'

'You're of age, Whitney. It's none of his business.'

'That might be true, if he were only my brother. But he's also my boss.'

'Your work isn't suffering.'

Whitney felt a brief pang of guilt. It was a good thing Max didn't know how many times during these last few days her thoughts had drifted away from Tyler-Royale and on to him! It frightened her, and she didn't quite know what to do about it. But it would panic Max, the free spirit, if he knew...

'Besides,' she said, in an attempt to sidetrack the argument. 'You'll be out of town next week, and I'll have enough trouble moving everything back here to the hotel without adding any more to it.'

Max shrugged. 'Why? You could still stay there. I don't care if you use my house, and you're much happier when you're there.'

She shook her head. How could she tell him, she wondered, that it was he who made her glow with contentment? How could she dare to take the risk he asked of her? To move her possessions into his home—how easy it would be, then, to forget that they were only playing house. So long as her belongings stayed at the hotel, at least she would have a little independence, and a reminder that things would not always be this way, that this was just a brief moment snatched from two separate lives.

As it was, their time together was quickly drawing to a close. It was like a pleasant dream that was beginning to fray around the edges, as dreams did sometimes in the early morning when she was half-awake, half-asleep, not wanting to return to consciousness but knowing that the pleasantness that surrounded her was not real. She had tried for days to forget that in another week or two there would be a new manager at Tyler-Royale's Kansas City store, and Whitney Lattimer would move on to the next trouble-spot.

Just remember, Whitney, she warned herself, that this cannot last. Don't kid yourself. This is a moment seized out of two separate lifetimes, and when it's over, we'll both go on our separate ways.

It had been less than a week since that first magical night had shattered her certainties and shown her the power of desire. She would never forget what she had learned here, about herself, about passion, about gentleness.

Would Max remember, too, she wondered. Or would he put her out of his mind with relief? Was he looking forward to the time when she would be gone, and he would be free? Sometimes, in the last few days, she had looked up and caught him watching her, and wondered what was going on in his mind. Sometimes he looked so unhappy that she could scarcely bear it. But as soon as he saw that she had noticed, his smile would flash, and he would make a teasing remark, or kiss her, and the moment when she could have asked what he was thinking would be gone.

Be honest, Whitney, she told herself. You wouldn't ask, because you don't want to know. You can't face knowing.

There was a pain in the pit of her stomach at the thought that he might be anxious for her to go.

And I refuse to think about that tonight, she told herself. I'm going to have fun tonight. Tonight, I can still pretend that Max belongs to me——

The glow of candles filled the great hall of the old mansion. The marble floor, polished to a gleam, was perfect for dancing. The chamber orchestra was seated on the huge landing above, and the soft strains of violins floated through the house. In the dining-room were tables loaded with food—patty shells filled with lobster salad, tiny sandwiches stuffed with dozens of delicious fillings, champagne punch served from a silver bowl so highly polished that the delicate weave of the linen cloth formed a visual pattern on its smooth surface.

Yes, Whitney thought as she descended the main staircase, these people really knew how to throw a party. In two hours she had met more of Kansas City's elite than she had known existed.

They had all been so friendly that it had startled her. It was an informal and casual city, she had found, more like a small town in many ways. Or was that only because she was with Max?

For every one of these people knew Max—and not only knew him, but greeted him with easy familiarity and even with curiosity about who his companion was. Their curiosity hadn't surprised her, though she would have expected that if these people knew Max at all, they certainly couldn't have been shocked at him turning up with an unknown woman. But she had been a little surprised that Max actually fitted in a place like this. Max belonged to the smooth modern world of glass and steel buildings, of retail wizardry, glossy advertising, and scientific methods. The Candlelight Ball was an evening from another century. And yet Max seemed to fit in perfectly...

Max, she thought as she reached the landing and looked out across the great hall below, full of people and chatter and laughter. Her mind seemed to be running in circles tonight; every times she tried to think of something else, she came back automatically to Max.

She looked out over the mass of people as she started down the main flight of steps, and saw him immediately. He was off in a corner, away from the crowd, almost as if he didn't want to be observed. Odd, how she had picked him out automatically, she thought. He was neither the tallest nor the most handsome man present. And there must be a couple of hundred men in the hall, most wearing the standard black of formal evening clothes. Here and there a daring male sported white, or cream, or grey. She had even seen one portly man in burgundy. But, like most of them, Max was wearing black—and yet her eyes had gone straight to him, as if there were no other man in the room.

Not surprising, she told herself with a secret little smile, recalling the way that he could walk into a room and within two minutes remove every concern but him from her mind. It seemed as though, no matter where he was, he drew her attention irresistibly.

As did the woman he was talking to, she realised abruptly. She was a beautiful woman, Whitney thought, though from this distance, she didn't even know what made her so certain. She thought it might be the way the woman stood, as if she had never questioned her own attractiveness. Her back was turned to Whitney, and her dress, a billowy cloud of white, left her shoulders bare. As Whitney watched from the steps, the woman put a hand possessively on Max's arms, and Whitney was conscious of an illogical disappointment when he didn't pull away.

Who is she, Whitney wondered? A client, perhaps? A friend? A former lover?

And why, Whitney asked herself irritably, should it matter in the least to me?

But it did matter. Suddenly, it mattered horribly. The very thought of Max with this woman—with any woman—was like an arrow to her heart.

That's insane, Whitney, she told herself, furious at the very idea that she could be jealous over Max. Somebody had to have taught him all those lovely gestures he's practised on you all week. You should be grateful, not jealous . . .

But she still wanted to scratch the woman's eyes out.

Whitney reached the foot of the stairs and skirted the dance-floor, where couples were moving slowly to the soft strains of a popular love-song. Max saw her coming. He said something to his companion, but the woman did not turn around. What was it, Whitney wondered. Was he confiding that Whitney was only a social project, his little contribution towards improving the world?

As she came closer, she found her original assessment confirmed. The woman was beautiful. The straight spine, the perfect creamy skin, the way her dark hair lifted off a slender neck and flowed into a smooth knot at her crown——

Oh, stop it! Whitney told herself furiously. You can't walk through the rest of the evening wondering which of these women he might have slept with. It can't make a single bit of difference to you! It startled her to realise that she had been doing precisely that.

Maybe she's concerned about me, too, Whitney thought. She might actually be worried. And then a drop of sympathy for the woman bubbled up in her. Would she herself glance up some day, with her hand on Max's arm, and find him looking at another woman? A younger woman, perhaps, or a prettier one?

Don't be ridiculous, Whitney, she lectured herself. It's not as if you expected this to be any lasting thing. Max made that perfectly clear from the outset. You won't even be here to see another woman beside him. That thought didn't help at all.

Max stretched out a hand to take Whitney's. 'I thought you'd got lost on the stairs,' he said.

I'll just bet, she thought. You were enjoying yourself. 'Are you going to introduce me, Max? Or shall I have to do it myself?'

He raised an eyebrow, and Whitney would have given anything to snatch the words back. There had been a tart note in her voice, as if she had the right to demand anything from him. Suddenly, she felt like crying.

The woman laughed and turned, with one hand still on Max's sleeve. For the first time, Whitney saw her face. It was Cindy Bell.

'Hello, Mrs Lattimer,' she said cheerfully. 'Didn't you recognise me without my clipboard?'

Whitney's knees threatened to give way. She would have liked to ooze through the nearest crack in the marble floor and vanish. A waiter passed just then, and she took advantage of the tray of champagne glasses to cover her shock. 'I didn't, as a matter of fact, Cindy,' she admitted. My God, she was thinking, I can't be jealous of Cindy Bell!

Cindy had heard the note of strain in her voice, that was apparent. Concern flared in her eyes. 'Max,' she said, 'go and get me a shrimp puff, would you?'

'What a way to treat your employer,' he grumbled.

'You're not my employer tonight.'

'Well, what do you have a husband for, anyway?'

'If you see him, tell him where I am.' Gently, she urged him towards the dining-room. As soon as he walked off, still grumbling, she turned to Whitney. 'Are you all right, Mrs Lattimer?'

Whitney looked at the bottom of her champagne glass. 'I'm fine,' she said.

There was a momentary silence. The orchestra began to play again. Cindy Bell said, 'Don't let him see how jealous you are.'

'Jealous!' Whitney laughed a little, brittly. She refused to meet Cindy's sympathetic eyes.

'There are some men whom every woman would like to mother,' Cindy said thoughtfully, 'because they have such charm. Max is one of them. But that doesn't mean that every woman who would like to pamper him succeeds.' Just what did that mean, Whitney wondered. 'But I've never seen him quite like this before.'

'I'm afraid I don't understand——'

Cindy interrupted her and said, lightly. 'Of course, Max delights in outraging society.'

It seemed that the moment of confidence was past. 'Does that mean that he doesn't do this sort of thing regularly?' Whitney's gesture drew in the whole room.

'This is the first event of this kind that he's attended in a year.' Cindy took a shrimp puff from the plate that Max handed her. 'In fact,' she said, as though he wasn't standing right beside her, 'when he called me at home and asked me to get two tickets for him, I almost concluded that it was a prank call and ignored it.' She smiled sweetly up at him. 'Thanks, Max.'

'So he's not a playboy after all,' Whitney mused.

Cindy's eyes flashed with amusement. 'You've got it.' Her tone said far more than the words. 'I think I'd better see what sort of trouble my husband is in by now,' she murmured, and moved away, the white cloud of her dress bright in the dim room.

What was she really telling me, Whitney wondered. That I don't need to be jealous? That it would do me no good to be? That if Max realises I am, he'll drop me instantly?

'It's so nice that I have a fan-club,' Max mused. 'Let's dance.'

She moved automatically into his arms, still thinking about what Cindy had said. Don't let him see that you're jealous—— Fine to say that, she thought, but just what was she to do about it? How strange that abrupt flash of jealousy had been, anyway. She had tensed clear to her bones at the very idea that this unknown woman might be closer to Max than she could ever be. Whitney had never thought of herself as a jealous person; the sudden flare-up of the monster had taken her by surprise.

She nestled a little closer to Max, who put his cheek down against her hair. She fell silent, listening to the strong beat of the music, letting her feet move automatically. How comfortable she was in his arms, how safe and protected, wrapped in the blanket of music and warmth, and Max. Nothing could hurt her, nothing could intrude, so long as she stayed here in the arms of the man she loved...

She tested the word, tentatively, in her thoughts. Love. I love Max. I've fallen in love with Max...

It came as no surprise. There was a twinge of sadness, but no amazement. She must have known it, in the back of her mind, for days. It would be so easy to fall in love with him, she had told herself that first night, and she had been right. She had done exactly that.

And Max, she told herself firmly, must never know.

Two more weeks, she thought wearily. That was all she could count on, all the time she would have to spend with this man she had come to care so very much about. And one of those weeks Max would spend out of town on a business trip...

You will survive, Whitney, she told herself firmly. You survived Charles——

She had almost forgotten, she realised in wonder. The hurt and the heartbreak of her time with Charles had receded, healed by her love for Max.

But what if her love for Max carried a hurt with it as well?

You will survive that, too, she told herself, because you must. There was no backing out now; she had gone too far.

She moved a little closer to him, and tried to memorise the sound of his heart beating, the smell of his aftershave, the slickness of the satin lapel of his jacket against her cheek. These were all the things that would be left to her, in another couple of weeks. She knew that she had to learn them well, for the memories would have to keep her warm.

CHAPTER TEN

WHITNEY stood beside the kitchen window, staring out unseeingly across the wide lawn where patches of green grass struggled to fight off the approaching winter, where oak leaves cast golden shadows across the driveway, where the crisp autumn sunshine of early morning lay in warm patches across ground where frost had rested just an hour before.

It ought to be raining, she thought. The sun shouldn't be allowed to shine on a day like this—a day that would mark the end of so many things. On a day like this, it should be just as gloomy and dull and cold and bitter outside as it was in her heart.

She glanced at her wristwatch. Max was still upstairs packing; in less than two hours, he had to check in at the airport. He would fly to Detroit, where he would spend all week making a report to the president of a food company on the nation's attitude towards cornflakes—or something just about as exciting; she didn't know exactly what was involved. And Whitney would be left alone in Kansas City.

You're acting as if it's the end of the world, she accused herself irritably. You know that in another week, or two at the most, you'll be on your own again, without Max. You'll go back to Chicago, and Max will stay here, and your glorious little interlude will be over.

It's already tarnished around the edges, she reminded herself. Impatience had crept in here and there, and dimmed the magic glow a little. And they had had their first sharp words yesterday. They had both been tired from the Candlelight Ball, they had said, and they had apologised. But it was apparent to anyone with eyes that the glory was diminishing.

And that, of course, was what was making her the saddest of all.

The coffee finished perking, and she turned from the window and poured herself a cup.

'Idiot,' she accused herself under her breath. 'You'd like to pretend that he'll be coming home to you in a few days, and that it will be like this for ever, all sunshine and love and Max and Whitney together.'

Well, wake up and smell the roses, sweetheart, she thought. Oh, he would come home, all right, and if Whitney was still in Kansas City, there would no doubt be another pleasant series of passionate nights, another set of lessons in the art of love.

Love, she thought bitterly. How was it possible that she had fallen in love, so deeply and so hopelessly? It wasn't Max's fault, that was sure. He had made no promises, had held out no hopes. And yet she had tumbled into this madly chaotic emotion that left her spinning wildly from happiness to despair, from jealousy to trust——

No, it wasn't Max's fault. It wasn't hers either, really. But it could only end in her being hurt worse than she had ever been hurt before.

Unless, she thought, she was smart enough to end it now. It was a hopeless situation; all that she could accomplish by hanging on was to increase her own pain. It would be over soon, no matter what; Ross would find a new manager any day now, and she would be summoned back to Chicago.

But what if Ross didn't find a new manager? Then she could stay, and she and Max—— The sudden burst of happiness was like a sunbeam in her heart.

If I can just stay with him, she thought, the rest doesn't matter. I don't care if he marries me. Marriage isn't important.

Then reality returned. You say that the legal formalities aren't important, she accused herself, but you would consider yourself married, and you want Max to feel the same. And that's exactly what Max has said he would never do. He will not be tied down, with or without a wedding ring.

She stared out of the window at a squirrel who was trying to climb the oak tree with an apple in his mouth. The fruit was far too big for him to hold. He lost his grip, and the apple bounced to the ground and rolled across the lawn. The squirrel dashed down after it, nibbled a bite or two to keep his strength up and to make it easier to get a grip, then started up the tree again. The weight of the apple made it look as if he was climbing in slow motion.

'Give it up,' Whitney advised. 'It's too much for you to handle.'

Good advice, she told herself. The situation with Max was becoming too much for her to handle, as well. Not that she hadn't benefited, she admitted. She had learned a great deal from Max—that she did indeed have a strong and passionate nature, that she could overcome the hurts of the past and live again, that she had a great deal to offer a man.

And what good does all that do me, she thought bitterly, when I learned it by falling in love with a man who intended only to do me a favour?

Don't ever kid yourself, she warned sternly, that this time with you has meant anything more than a vacation to Max. When it's time for you to say goodbye, he'll wave you off with a smile, and you won't be out of sight before he's calling another girl.

Why, she wondered, why did I have to fall in love with him?

Innate honesty provided the answers. Because he was kind to you, she told herself. And gentle. And because he's charming, and good-looking, and he has a great sense of humour, and he's a wonderful lover, and——

Max came into the kitchen quietly. 'I can't get my cufflinks in,' he said. 'Help me?'

And because he needs someone to look after him, Whitney thought. It was the quality Cindy had pointed out.

As long as Max breathes, she told herself, there will be a dozen women willing to supply that care. So don't let yourself be fooled into thinking that he depends on you for it!

She slid the gold cufflinks in and straightened his tie.

'Thanks, hon,' he said, and kissed the tip of her nose, but his heart didn't seem to be in the gesture.

He was already thinking about the work waiting for him in Detroit, she thought sadly. It was as if there had been no night before, when he had held her and made love to her till almost dawn.

'I forgot to give you this last night.' He dropped a brass key into her hand. 'That's to the side door,' he said.

'For the house?' She looked at the dull shine of it in her palm.

'No silly, for the convention centre. Of course it's for the house. You'll have to get in and out somehow while I'm gone.'

She shook her head. 'I'm not staying here, Max.'

He had turned to the coffee-pot. Now he swung around and said, 'We've been over all this before, Whitney. Stop being so damned inflexible.'

They had been over lots of things, she thought wearily. 'Well, you may have gone over all this, but I only listened. I certainly never agreed to move in here. And if I'm being inflexible, Max, you're being callous to ignore my feelings about it.'

'Staying here is the only sensible thing for you to do.'

'I have a perfectly good hotel suite, or have you forgotten?'

'And you hate the thing. Why not be comfortable here?'

Because I can't stand the thought of being here without you, she reflected. Because every chair, every cup, every towel reminds me of you. Because if I stay here while you're gone, it will be far too easy to convince myself that I belong here, and that you think so too——

Tears threatened. I cannot cry, she told herself fiercely. I cannot let him see me cry.

'Why are you so anxious for me to stay, Max?' she asked nastily. 'Do you want to be sure I'm here waiting for your convenience when you get home?'

His eyes narrowed. 'That was low.'

'It seemed a logical conclusion to me.' She saw anger rising in his eyes, and prudently changed her tone. 'Really, Max. What would the girls in the office think?'

'They have nothing to do with it, dammit! They know better than to consider it their business——'

'I'll just bet they do,' Whitney said sweetly. 'It was silly of me to be concerned about them. After all, they've had plenty of experience.'

He stared down at her, and then said, his voice icy, 'Yes, there have been other women in my life! If you wouldn't behave like a baby about it——'

'*I'm* behaving like a baby? You're the one who's throwing a temper tantrum because you aren't getting your own way.'

'I only want you to be comfortable while I'm gone, Whitney.'

'Good. Then I'll stay at the hotel, with your approval.' She put the brass key firmly into his hand. 'Max, I think you need to realise that I am capable of taking care of myself, and that it's really none of your business what I do.'

He stared down at the key and said tartly, 'Staying here for a few days doesn't mean you'd be moving in permanently, you know.' It was like a slap in the face. He seemed to realise it, and said, more softly, 'Are you afraid of being alone here?'

She hesitated. It had never occurred to her to be afraid to stay alone in the big house; she had been alone so much in her life, and she had grown fond of the house.

How very much she had come to like this warm kitchen—
and how much she dreaded that hotel suite! But she could
not stay here with the memories, and allow herself to
think of how wonderful it would be if only he *had* asked
her to move in permanently.

She hardened her heart. 'That's all I have to say, Max.
I'm not staying here.'

His dark gaze was unreadable. He turned the key over
in his hand, and then dropped it into his pocket. 'In that
case, it's time to leave for the airport, Whitney.'

She blinked, and swallowed hard. Somehow, she had
expected him to argue, to tell her that it *was* his business,
that he cared about her——

Foolish, she told herself wearily. Very, very foolish of
you, even to hope for that.

The drive to the airport was silent. Whitney's throat
was too choked to risk saying a word. Max seemed sim-
ilarly disinclined to talk. The miles seemed to take for
ever.

This is stupid, she thought suddenly as the car sped
down the freeway. It's over now; that's what has really
been happening. There's no sense in hanging on to
something that is already shattered, waiting for the in-
evitable end.

He seemed to read her mind. 'Don't bother with
parking the car,' he said. 'Just pull up to the terminal.
I'll get out there.'

She obeyed, silently. He reached into the back seat
for his briefcase and bag. 'See you Friday,' he said.
'Seven in the evening.'

He didn't ask if she would be there to pick him up,
she noticed. Was he so sure of her? 'I'll make sure
someone is here, Max.'

He looked puzzled. 'That's only five days,' he pointed
out. 'Surely you'll still be in Kansas City.'

'I haven't talked to Ross for a couple of days. He might
have found someone to take over the store.' She wouldn't
look at him.

'Even if he sent someone right now, you'd still be here Friday. Dammit, Whitney,' he ordered, 'at least be honest with me!'

She sighed. 'All right, Max, I will. I won't be coming to pick you up. It's over.'

There was a long silence. 'I see,' he said quietly. 'Spare me the bit about it being great fun, and all that.'

'Very well,' she said. 'Though I wasn't going to say it.'

'I don't understand this, you know.'

'I just think we should say goodbye now. There is no sense in stretching it out—we both know that in another week or so I'll be leaving anyway.'

'But we could have that week.' He didn't look at her.

And what would we do with it, she asked herself. Quarrel? Why not admit right now that the happy-ever-after has slipped away?

When she didn't answer, he went on, 'And this is what you want, Whitney?'

Of course not, she thought. But it's all I can have, and keep a few shreds of dignity. She smiled, painfully. 'Yes, Max,' she said. 'Thank you. You're a wonderful teacher, you know, and I'll never forget everything you've done for me.'

He slammed the car door without a word. Whitney winced at the sound, and drove off without waiting for him to enter the terminal. From the way he was acting, she wondered if it was the first time that he hadn't been the one to call a halt to an affair. She wouldn't be surprised. And if so, perhaps it would be good for him to know how it felt.

No, she thought. All it proved was that Max wasn't ready for this enjoyable game to be over. He might have had some other lessons planned for her——

Coldness settled like an ice-blanket around her heart. She had burned her bridges, and she would never again feel the warmth of his hands against her skin, or the soft brush of his breath against her cheek as he slept. All that was gone for ever.

'And I don't regret a moment of it,' Whitney told herself firmly. It had been a week of beauty that would be rare in her life. How could she wish to change even an instant of what they had shared? 'But I'm relieved that it's over,' she said, 'relieved that the goodbyes aren't still hanging over my head.'

And perhaps, she told herself gloomily, if she kept saying that often enough, eventually she would come to believe it.

Ross called at mid-morning. 'Where in the heck have you been?' he asked curiously.

Whitney considered saying, 'I was sleeping with your best friend,' just to find out how he would take the news. But the shock value wasn't worth having to explain it all—especially now that there would never be a need to explain—so instead she said, 'I was sightseeing.'

'All weekend?' Ross's voice was dry. 'Tell me, Whitney, what's open in Kansas City between two and four o'clock on a Sunday morning?'

'You tried to call me then?'

'Why not? I was up anyway, because the baby wanted to walk the floor. And since you hadn't been home at midnight, I didn't think you'd mind if I called at two. Just where the hell were you, anyway? I was worried.'

'Do you ask your other managers where they spend their off-duty time?' Whitney snapped.

There was a brief silence, then Ross, taken aback, said, 'No. But you are my sister. What's eating you?'

'Just that it's none of your business what I do, that's all. I'm a grown woman.'

'I know.' Ross said drily. 'Sometimes that's what worries me.'

'Well, if you want to know so badly, do your mind-reading act,' Whitney recommended.

'Pardon me for living,' Ross said sweetly.

Whitney was instantly contrite. It certainly wasn't Ross's fault that she was in a bad mood. 'I'm sorry I snapped at you. It's just that Kansas City is getting on my nerves. Have you found my replacement yet?'

'That's what I'm calling about. I think we're off the hook.'

Whitney sat up straight. There was a catch in her throat, and she wasn't quite sure if it was relief or despair. It's relief, she told herself firmly. It has to be relief, because I won't let it be despair!

'The assistant manager in Seattle has a girlfriend who's just graduating from medical school. She's applied for an internship at a hospital there in Kansas City, so he wants a transfer.'

'An assistant manager?' She knew she sounded doubtful, and she hated herself for even bringing it up, because it might risk her escape. But the words were already out. 'Can he cope with it, Ross? This store is a handful right now.'

'So what else do you suggest I do? I have you down there threatening to mutiny, and I could really use you in Los Angeles at the moment——'

'The assistant manager it is.' She tapped her pen on the desk blotter. 'But Ross, can you find someone else to take care of Los Angeles? I really don't want to travel any more.'

'Not today, Whitney. Please don't tell me this today.'

'I'm sorry. But that's the way I feel.' The nights in hotel rooms, alone in unfamiliar cities, with nothing to do but think—I'd go crazy with another month of it, she thought, if I lasted that long. 'I've grown to like managing the store, and——'

'Wait a minute. Just a darn minute, Whitney. Are you telling me you want to stay there after all?'

'Not in Kansas City. But I would like to have a store of my own, and be a little more settled somewhere.'

There was an awful, aching silence. 'I don't believe what I'm hearing. I've spent the last three weeks trying to rescue you from that store and now you want to stay?'

'That is not what I said.' Panic had started to set in. 'You wouldn't leave me down here, would you?'

'At the moment,' Ross said acidly, 'I've got more managers for Kansas City than I know what to do with.'

'I'd take Seattle,' Whitney offered. At least it would be far from Max, she thought, and perhaps it would help her to forget.

'You actually want to stop travelling?'

'Why not?' Whitney asked tartly. 'You quit, and you're enjoying having a store of your own. Isn't there someone besides me who can handle the excitement of living out of a suitcase for three weeks at a time?'

'Why don't we talk about this next week when you're back in Chicago?'

'The new manager will be here that soon?'

'He could be there by Friday.'

Friday, she thought. Max is coming back on Friday. That means I won't see him again at all... She swallowed hard. That's what you want, you fool, she told herself fiercely.

'You'll have to spend a few days helping him to get oriented to the store, of course,' Ross went on, 'but you'll be home next week some time. Does that sound good?'

She had forgotten that she couldn't just turn over the keys. A sense of dismay swept over her. Another weekend here—alone—knowing that Max was just blocks away?

'If the new manager doesn't mind working weekends,' she said, 'neither do I. That way I can leave here on Monday.'

'Don't push it, Whit. Don't waste the three weeks you've spent down there just because you're anxious for home.'

Ross would never understand, she thought, that her anxiety was not to get back to Chicago, but to escape. Home would be a retreat, a cave she could crawl into

and lick her wounds and assess what she had learned
from the last few weeks.

'I won't take that chance,' she said finally, reluctantly. 'I'll stay as long as I have to. The store comes
first. It always has, Ross, and it always will.'

She put the telephone down and pulled a stack of
letters across the blotter from the corner of her desk
where Georgia had left them. But instead of signing
them, she sat unseeing, staring at the crisp buff sta-
tionery with its dark brown printing listing the locations
of all the Tyler-Royale stores, and thinking that, in the
past, the store had come first with her because she loved
it so. In the future, however, it would be the primary
thing in her life because there was nothing else.

That's a stupid thing to say, she told herself. The store
is not the only thing; surely she had learned that much
from the whole affair with Max. It had taught her that
she didn't have to be crippled for life because of Charles;
surely if she could fall in love with Max, then some day
there would be another man she could care for——

Her heart rebelled at the very thought. After living
with Max for those brief days, laughing with him,
making love with him, how could she even consider
putting another man in his place?

She put her head down on the blotter. 'You're an idiot,
Whitney Lattimer,' she told herself uncompromisingly.
'You're a full-fledged idiot to have got yourself into this.'
And yet, she could not quite persuade herself to regret
the days and nights when Max had been the centre of
her world. At least she was alive again, and not that
frozen, half-conscious being who had wandered un-
feeling through the long days.

And as soon as she got away from Kansas City,
perhaps into a store of her own, she could begin to act
on those lessons that Max had taught so well. She could
look for new friends, ones who would accept her as she
was, and not for what she could give them. And some

day, perhaps when she wasn't even looking, another man would cross her path.

It sounded good. The trouble was, she couldn't quite make herself believe it.

Karen Emerson put her head in the door a little later. 'If you don't have a date, how about joining me for lunch?' she asked.

I don't think I'll ever feel hungry again, Whitney thought. But she hadn't talked to Karen in almost a week. 'Sure,' she said.

'I'm only going down to the Terrace,' Karen said. 'It's all I have time for. Some day I'm going to talk to the store manager and see if we can't arrange for longer lunch hours around here.' She said it with a smile.

'Wait till next week. It wouldn't do any good if I made the switch, anyway.'

The escalator delivered them to the doorway of the Terrace restaurant. Karen waited till they had been seated at a side table for two. Then she leaned across and said, 'And just what does that mean? You're the boss.'

'The new permanent manager will be here soon.'

Karen groaned. 'That's what I was afraid of. The grapevine has been saying that you were just temporary, but I was hoping that Ross would let you stay. Things have been going so well!'

Whitney shrugged. 'There is a lot further to go. And really, Karen, I've done my job.'

'Have you? The atmosphere has improved, I'll grant you. But a lot of that is because the staff trust you. How long is that going to last when you're gone and we have someone new that we know nothing about?'

'Karen, I think that anyone coming in could have done what I did.'

'Then you're severely underrating yourself, Whitney. You have a reputation in this chain. Everybody wanted to work up to your standards. But if you walk out now——'

'Really, Karen, that's hardly a fair way to put it. I am not walking out.'

'You said yourself in your first little pep-talk that no one should desert the ship because it looked as if it might sink. Now you're doing it.'

'I am not! My job is done, and I'm moving on——'

'I know that, Whitney. But most of the employees of this store aren't going to see it that way. They're going to think that you've written us off, and that Ross is sending someone else in here to mop up the leftovers and close the store. And with them thinking that, it's bound to happen.'

'I have full confidence in the new manager,' Whitney said stiffly, uncomfortably aware that it wasn't true.

'Who is he? One of the young hotshots?'

Whitney sighed. 'I can't tell you until it's official. But he's the assistant manager of one of the bigger stores.'

'Oh, really?' Karen's voice was dry. 'And we're his first experiment at handling his own store? That gives me the shivers.'

'Ross has confidence in him.'

'Well, pardon me, dear, but even if Ross thinks the man can make the sun rise in the west, it won't keep this store alive if the employees don't believe in him.'

'I suppose you have a point.'

'Of course I do. I've worked with these people.'

Whitney was tired of being on the defensive. She stirred her coffee and said, sweetly, 'That's why I think you should go in for manager-training, Karen. You have a great deal of insight when it comes to employee relations.'

Karen sighed. 'Unfortunately,' she said, 'there are some things I'm just not willing to sacrifice for the sake of a career.'

'And your boyfriend is one of them.'

'Really, Whitney, do you blame me? I'd have to be a fool to ask him to wait a year or two while I train. And even then I don't know where I'd be going. He's got a good position here. I can't ask him to give that up for the sake of a job I'm not even certain I'd like.'

'I know.' Whitney stared down into the clear brown depths of her cup, and suddenly realised that Max's eyes were the precise shade of well brewed coffee. Here we go again, she thought as she felt the familiar fluttering of her stomach. Back on the rollercoaster, thinking about Max—would it ever ease?

She understood Karen's decision, and she could not quarrel with it. I'd give up anything for Max, she thought wearily, if only Max wanted me to. If I could choose between Max and everything else in the world—job, career, family—I'd choose, Max, with or without promises, with or without a future. But that choice had never been hers to make. And now, after what she had said to him at the airport that morning, it was too late to make any choice at all.

If there really was a store somewhere called Heart's Desire, she thought, a store with the power to make one's dreams come true, she would walk in now and put her soul on the line, and say, 'I want Max Townsend——'

Just how many other women, she asked herself wearily, would make the same request?

And if there really was a Heart's Desire, what would Max himself be shopping for?

She thought a lot about what Karen had said over the next two days. She had plenty of time to think, in the silence of the hotel suite. She knew, the more that she thought about it, that Karen was right. No assistant manager, no matter how brilliantly he had performed his job, could work the miracles that would still be necessary to pull the Kansas City store through. Karen firmly believed that Whitney could; Whitney herself was less sure.

In any case, she decided, they would never find out. The new man would have to work the miracles, if there were to be any, because Whitney wasn't going to stay around to try.

As the week went on, she became even more certain that her decision had been the right one, for herself at least, if not for the store.

She had hoped, on Monday evening, that perhaps Max would call. She even ordered room-service, and hated herself for being weak enough to stay there and wait for him to call, instead of going out somewhere to find lights and music and people. But the telephone had remained stubbornly silent.

By Tuesday, she knew better than to wait. Max wasn't going to call; she had put a finish to the affair, and there was nothing more to say about it. The silent pair of rooms was driving her wild, and the isolation was more than she could bear. So she went, alone, to the rooftop restaurant where Max had taken her on her first night in the city.

That, too, was a mistake. She pushed the veal Parmesan around on her plate and finally gave up on the idea of eating.

It was no part of her plan to go anywhere close to Max's house, and yet she found herself there that night, sitting in the car at the end of the drive, watching the old brick house under the waning moonlight.

The house had seen generations come and go, she thought. It had survived war, and gloried in peace. It had watched families be born, grow up, and go out into the world. All those people loved and hated, wanted and sometimes were denied. How silly it was to feel this wrenching ache because she couldn't have what she wanted—as though she were the only person who had ever felt that way!

Chastened, she went back to the hotel. That night, she even slept a little. In her sleep, she hugged her pillow, and dreamed that it was Max.

* * *

By Friday morning, the store's grapevine had thoroughly spread the news that Whitney would be leaving soon, and that the new manager might be turning up at any hour. Where that information had come from, Whitney didn't know; she hadn't even told Karen. Someone must have a contact in the anchor store, she decided.

Even the confectionery department manager seemed less than pleased at the idea of her going. When she stopped at the counter on Friday morning and asked for a quarter-pound of fudge, he weighed it out carefully without a smile, handed it morosely over the counter and waved away the cash she offered.

'This one's on me,' he said, and pulled his wallet out.

'You can't make a profit that way,' Whitney said, trying to get a teasing note into her voice as she quoted his own wisdom at him.

'No?' He cocked an eyebrow. 'You'd be surprised how many old biddies—sorry, Mrs Lattimer—how many ladies came in to buy things this week and mentioned that Miss Meadows told them how personal the service is here. Come to think of it, I don't imagine you'd be surprised at all, would you?'

'Not really.' Whitney tried to smile.

'Well, if you could just do for the rest of the store what you did for this department——'

'I've tried. And now the new manager will be taking over.'

The man frowned. 'But why?' he asked fiercely. 'You were just hitting your stride. I thought you liked the store, and that you wanted it to succeed——'

'I do. I hope very much that this store will survive. But I have other responsibilities as well.'

A customer stepped up to the counter just then, and Whitney moved away. It was just as well that they had been interrupted, she thought. There would have been no convincing the man. Karen had been right, she thought. The employees would not easily put their con fidence in the new manager. It would take longer than she had expected to make the transition. And no matter how sincere the new man was, the change might be the final blow—the death of this store.

She went to her office, unwrapped the fudge, and thoughtfully ate two pieces of it while she considered the problem.

I want to get away from this place, she thought. But I do owe my first loyalty to Tyler-Royale, and I think Ross should be warned about this. It's not my imagination; this is real.

But what do I do if he asks me to stay here, she wondered. How can I handle that? What if I have to see Max——

Then you'll see him, she told herself firmly. And you'll be grateful for what he taught you, and that will be the end of it. And if, perhaps, Max wanted more than that——

She closed her eyes against the tears, but the hot drops squeezed through and caught in her dark lashes.

'Then I'll do whatever he wants,' she whispered painfully. 'Whatever his terms, for whatever time——'

Hope dies hard and cruelly, she told herself. It was far more likely that Max would avoid her, and save her the trouble of staying out of his way.

It would be stupid of her to call Ross now, she argued. The new manager might very well be landing at the airport right now! She could hardly greet him at the door and tell him that he wasn't wanted or needed any longer. And yet——

Before she could argue herself out of it, she picked up the telephone.

Ross was out of his office, and his secretary had to search for him. While she waited, Whitney flipped through the mail that Georgia had left on her desk blotter and stopped at a Tyler-Royale envelope, hand-addressed to her and marked *Personal*. Who at the anchor store would be sending her hand-written letters, she asked herself idly? Ross did, now and then, when it wasn't company business, or when he didn't want to wait for his secretary. But the handwriting wasn't familiar.

It was a note from Pete Ward. 'I thought you'd like to know that my wife and I have got together again,' he had written. 'Now that it looks as if I'm still going to have a desk at Tyler-Royale, could you send me the things I left behind?'

She smiled and laid the letter aside. At least that bit of meddling had turned out well, she thought.

When Ross finally answered, Whitney could hear the familiar noises of the anchor store in the background, and sudden home-sickness almost made her reconsider her purpose.

'I thought you'd have called by now,' she said tentatively.

'I didn't have anything more to tell you, till this morning.'

'Anything definite on the new manager?'

'Do you want the good news or the bad news?' Ross sounded cheerful enough.

He's on his way, Whitney thought. Well, we'll make the best of it. Perhaps Ross will agree that I should stay a little while, at least.

'The good news first,' she said. 'I could stand some.'

'The good news is that the girlfriend got a wonderful internship. The bad news is that it's in Honolulu, and the man who was going to take over the Kansas City store has resigned from Tyler-Royale altogether and is going to guide busloads of tourists around the islands instead. At any rate, my dear——'

Her hand tightened on the edge of the desk. 'I'm stuck in Kansas City.'

'Whit, I'm sorry. I just found out this morning that he'd backed out. I'll send someone down to relieve you just as soon as I can——'

She paused, knowing that if she stayed silent now, it would all be over soon. She would be safely away, Max would be left behind, and the store——

I have to take care of the store, she thought.

'No, Ross,' she said, finally, and felt that she was taking charge of her own life for the first time in years. 'This is my store now. I'll take the responsibility for it from now on. When it's back in shape and making money, then we'll talk about what I do next.'

'Perhaps I ought to give you combat pay,' Ross said ruefully.

'Just give me time, and we'll pull through.'

'All the time you need. I have confidence in you, Whitney. And don't forget that you have Max. He'll help out all he can.'

'Right,' she said, and her voice was rock-steady. 'I know I can always depend on Max.'

Good old Max, she thought. The funny thing was that Ross would never know just how sincere she was with that promise! I won't ever forget Max, she thought. I could never forget Max...

CHAPTER ELEVEN

AND now, she thought, it was time to get down to business. The first thing, she decided, was to get her office in shape. Cleaning out the files and sending Pete Ward's belongings on to him would be a good start.

She opened a file drawer and sighed. She hadn't even looked at most of the things Pete had left behind; Whitney hadn't considered them to be top priority. The new manager could take care of all of that, she had thought—including cleaning out the desk drawers to make room for his own things.

Whitney had filled a waste-paper basket by the time Georgia brought her cup of coffee. 'Thanks, Georgia,' she said, and took a long sip. 'Do we have a box around here somewhere?'

'In a department store?' Georgia asked drily. 'Do you want a carton, a gift box, a fold-up container to wrap a shirt in, a crate that china was packed in, a——'

Whitney held up a defensive hand. 'Just a nice strong box about this size——' she gestured '—that I can send these things in.'

Georgia looked at the array of personal items on the corner of the desk and sighed. 'I'll go down to receiving and get a box,' she said. 'We're all very sorry to see you leave, Mrs Lattimer. I liked Mr Ward; that was no problem; but I trust you, somehow.'

Whitney smiled. 'Despite all the letters I made you write?'

'Oh, that wasn't so bad. And there's a whole different attitude about coming to work now. There's a delegation to see you, by the way. Shall I show them in before I go get the box?'

'A delegation of what?' Whitney asked doubtfully. 'I'm in the middle of a mess here.'

'Oh, they'll understand. It's just some of the employees.'

Whitney looked around at the piles of paper and folders, and sighed. 'Sure. Bring them in.'

There were half a dozen of them, including Karen Emerson and the confectionery department manager. They filed in and stood in a semicircle around Whitney's desk.

'What's this all about?' she asked.

'There will probably be a formal farewell party, but we all wanted to come and tell you what you've meant to the store,' Karen said. 'And to present you with this, as a small token of our respect for the best cheerleader this store has ever had.'

From behind his back, the confectionery department manager produced a large cardboard megaphone, painted in Tyler-Royale's buff and brown, with the chain's monogram on the side. He handed it solemnly across the desk to Whitney. 'We'd have brought the pompons too,' he said, 'but we couldn't find them in the right colours.'

'Be serious,' Karen told him sternly. 'Whitney, we hope that you'll continue to use that megaphone when you get back to Chicago, to let everybody in the head office know that we still intend to win this game.'

Whitney brushed a tear aside and thought, it must be something about the air in this city. I never used to cry until I came here! 'That's a really wonderful idea,' she said, 'and I have every intention of telling the people in the head office about the hard workers I have down here. But I think it will be important as a reminder to all of you, too—a reminder that I believe in you. So I think I'll hang it right here, so that every time you come in to see me——'

'You're staying?' Karen's tone was unbelieving.

Whitney nodded.

'Not just temporary?' The confectionery department manager sounded suspicious.

'Permanent manager,' Whitney said.

There were shrieks of delight, whistles, and something that resembled a cheer.

Whitney was horrified at the strength of their re-action. 'Look,' she protested, 'there is nothing magical about me. It's all of you who are doing the hard work——'

Karen nodded. 'That's the kind of statement that won you the megaphone,' she said. 'Keep it up and we'll get you the uniform for Christmas.'

'Speaking of Christmas,' Whitney said, 'it's coming faster than you think, and it's our best chance to pull this store out of the red. So hit those floors and get back to work pleasing customers!'

'Yes, ma'am.' The confectionery department man sa-luted, but there was a twinkle in his eyes.

They burst out of the office. One of them stopped Georgia, on her way in with an empty box, and hugged her. It won't take long for the grapevine to pass that news along, Whitney thought. It was just as well.

She held up the megaphone. Somebody had spent hours crafting it and painting it smooth. Now she had to live up to the trust they had put in her.

'Pack those things, Georgia,' she told the secretary. 'And then send them off to Pete—the head office has his address. I'll make a list of things for you to requis-ition for me next week.'

Georgia goggled. 'Then you're really staying? I'm so glad.'

The secretary's reaction left Whitney feeling that she could take on anything and win on a day like this. It was in that mood that she picked up the telephone and dialled the number of Max's office.

I'll tell Cindy that she doesn't need to pick Max up at the airport after all, she thought. I can be there at seven. And perhaps, if he isn't too tired, I could treat him to dinner for a change, and we can talk——

When she had called Cindy earlier in the week, Whitney had been afraid that the girl would start asking embarrassing questions. But Cindy hadn't. She had merely agreed to see that Max was met at the airport. She hadn't sounded pleased about it, though, so Whitney thought that Cindy probably wouldn't mind at all if the plans were changed.

'I'm sorry, Mrs Lattimer,' the receptionist said. 'Cindy took off early today.'

'Oh.' Whitney glanced at her watch. It was only mid-afternoon; plenty of time to rearrange things, if Whitney could only let her know! 'It's rather important, I'm afraid. Do you have her home number?'

'I believe she was going shopping.'

'That's a busman's holiday, isn't it?'

The receptionist laughed. 'It certainly is. Mr Townsend might know where to find her. Would you like to speak to him?'

Mr Townsend? Whitney's heart skipped a couple of beats before righting itself. Max was there, in the office? He had come back early, and not let her know?

'Is he there?' she asked, trying to keep her voice steady.

'Yes. I'll put you through.'

Whitney panicked. 'Oh, no. Don't bother him. He's busy, I'm sure, so soon after getting back from his trip.'

'He came back yesterday,' the receptionist volunteered. 'I'm sure he wouldn't mind, Mrs Lattimer—since it's you.'

'No.' She swallowed hard, and tried to steady her voice so that it didn't sound so frightened. 'I—it wasn't as important as I thought it was, after all.' She put the telephone down quietly.

Until that instant, she had never quite believed that it was over, she admitted to herself. She had assumed that Max had not argued with her that day on the way to the airport because there had been so little time to discuss it. She had believed that he had not called because he would rather talk about it in person.

And now he had come back—had been back in town for twenty-four hours—and instead of rushing right up to see her, he had not contacted her at all.

Well, that's that, she told herself. Be grateful for what you learned, and go on from there. You should be glad that you called a halt to it when you did. Now the hurt is past and you can start to heal. If you hadn't ended it, then you'd only be hurt worse in a week, or a month, or three months, when Max did the breaking off. You should feel fortunate that you had a lover like Max at all, and that you learned so much about yourself.

Dammit, I don't feel fortunate, she admitted painfully. Or glad. I wish with all my heart that I could be with him tonight, and every night.

But that was no longer an option. And it never would be, she told herself firmly. Only a fool would put herself back into that situation.

She spent the rest of the afternoon trying to convince herself that she was not a fool.

She bought a newspaper at the gift-shop and went up to her suite, determined to spend the weekend searching for somewhere to live. That would help, she thought, and dreamed of small, bright rooms lit by sunshine and decorated in warm pastels. No more dark green carpet for her, she thought, looking at the suite's floor in disgust. No more tropical-rain-forest curtains. No more fake Henry-the-Eighth-era plastic furniture. But neither would she be like Emma Meadows, surrounded by her thousands of knicknacks. Whitney would have light and air and delicate furniture and good taste. Perhaps a cat, she decided; now that she wouldn't be travelling all the time, she could manage a pet. She could talk to a cat, and then she wouldn't feel so terribly alone.

She stood in the doorway of the suite and fought off the loneliness that threatened to drag her down. A Persian, she decided, with determination. A fluffy white cat, with blue eyes. That would fit with the apartment she visualised.

Not the world's best reason to buy a cat, she reflected. Simply because he matches the decor!

It felt a little better, just knowing that her sense of humour hadn't died completely, she thought. She hung up her suit, wrapped herself in a comfortable old terry robe, and sat down at the table with the classified ads. There were columns of flats to let; surely it would not be hard to find what she wanted. Near the Plaza, she thought, so perhaps in good weather she could even walk to work. At least two bedrooms, so she would have a place for a small office. A small, neat kitchen...

She propped her chin on her hand and stared at the smudgy newsprint, and caught herself long minutes later thinking about Max's kitchen and how much she had liked it. Whitney had never been much of a cook, but there had been something about that kitchen that had encouraged her to try her hand at all sorts of new things.

She sighed, and went back to reading the ads, circling a promising one here and there.

When there was a knock at the door, she looked up, puzzled, and tried to remember if she had actually ordered her dinner from room-service or if she had merely been thinking about it.

'I'm going to have to work on this memory of mine,' she muttered as she went to answer the knock.

'What did I order?' she asked as she pulled the door open. Then her breath jerked to a halt in her throat. 'Max,' she managed to choke.

All the longing of the last five days without him welled up in her. She was afraid to look at him; she didn't think she could bear it if he saw the gladness and the pain in her eyes, and felt sorry for her.

'May I come in?' he asked.

She nodded. She couldn't trust herself to speak.

'I brought you the report on the survey information.' He closed the door behind him, and handed her a thick document.

It was bigger, and heavier, than she had expected. She hugged it to her as if it had been him. 'What does it show?'

Max shrugged. 'We didn't find any dramatic problems that will yield to easy solutions, that's certain. Bad management, of course, was the main thing. Not much that you didn't already know. I suppose you think it was a waste of time even to bring me into it.' It sounded like a challenge.

She shook her head, quietly.

'It will take someone a lot of time to straighten it out, Whitney,' he warned. 'It's no job for an amateur.'

'I know.'

'Ross should pick his manager very carefully.' He was being very careful not to look at her.

She realised suddenly that she wasn't exactly dressed right to receive guests, and she pulled the collar of the terry robe closer around her throat. It almost brought tears to her eyes, to think that Max no longer wanted to touch her, or even to look at her.

'How was Detroit?' she asked.

Max shrugged. 'I didn't see much of it. The hotel was nice.'

'They all are, for a while. Then you start getting tired of them.' She glanced at the report. 'I didn't expect you to bring this here.'

'I'm sorry if I've offended you.' His tone was tart.

'That wasn't what I meant, Max. You could have brought it to the store next week.'

'I wanted to give it to you personally.'

'I see.'

'You called the office today. I thought perhaps you were anxious to see the report.'

'It was nothing important.'

There was a brief, strained silence. This is stupid, Whitney thought. We're standing here like strangers, trying to make civil conversation! 'Well, thank you. It was kind of you to bring it by.'

'It was no problem.' His voice was curt, his movements almost jerky. 'Will you call me before you leave, Whitney?'

Her heart started to pound, and then she realised that he was anxious to see what she thought of the findings. 'Of course. I'll read the report this weekend and get back to you on Monday.'

He made a gesture, as if he would like to say something, and then he merely nodded.

I'd better tell him that I'm staying in Kansas City, she thought. Otherwise, when he hears the news, he may think that I'm staying because of him—that despite it all I expect that we'll be together. I don't want him to have the wrong impression.

She was still searching for the words when he moved towards the door and stopped beside the table where the classified section lay spread out, bits circled here and there. 'What's this?' he asked abruptly.

'Oh, I'm looking for an apartment.' Whitney tried to laugh. 'It's rather funny, actually. After all the fuss about finding another manager, Ross didn't have any luck at all. I'm stuck with the job for the next few months, at least.' No sense in telling him that it was permanent; he would eventually find that out for himself.

'You're staying?' His voice was only a hoarse croak.

She stared at his knuckles, white from strain where his hand clenched the back of a chair. She didn't dare to look at his face; she couldn't have borne to see the stress there.

He's afraid, she thought painfully. He's afraid of what I might say. 'I hope I'll see you now and then,' she said, choosing her words carefully and forcing herself to sound cheerful. 'I'm sure this report isn't the end of the work on the store. We'll need surveys and questionnaires in the future——' How much I want him, she thought. I'd forgotten, in these few days, how he can stand there and look at me and make me tremble with wanting him!

He didn't speak for a long time. Then he said, quietly, 'I'll be around.'

Whitney hurried on. 'You will help me, won't you, Max? You've done such a wonderful job for Tyler-Royale——'

'Oh, I'll help,' he interrupted. 'It's my job, after all.'

There was a twist to his words that flayed her heart, even though she didn't quite understand. She smothered the ache and nodded. 'I'll read the report tonight, Max.'

'I'll leave you to it, then.' He moved to the door, and stood there a moment, looking back at her as if there was something more he wanted to say. Then he turned the knob.

She was clenching her fists in the pockets of the robe to keep herself from holding out her arms to him. She even welcomed the physical pain because it helped to block the emotional one. But she couldn't help the strangled little cry she uttered, like a heartbroken child. 'Max——'

At the same instant, he shut the door and turned to face her. 'I can't let it rest this way,' he said. 'I have to know. Whitney, where did we go wrong?' It was an urgent question, taut, as if it hurt him to ask.

She looked up into his eyes, the colour of black coffee just now. I broke the rules, she almost said. I broke the rules and fell in love with you. I couldn't play the game—that's where we went wrong, Max.

But she was afraid to say those things, afraid of what his answer would be. I want to remember him as a strong and tender man who cared about me, she thought. I don't want my last memory of him to be as a hunted, unhappy man, trying to tell me as gently as he can that he only wanted to have an affair with me...

'I don't know, Max,' she whispered.

The silence was like that before a thunderstorm, when electricity saturates the air. His hand fell on her shoulder, and pulled her around to face him.

'Damn it,' Max said. 'I'm not taking that as an answer, Whitney. You know what it was. You have to know! Damn it, where did I go wrong? What did I do to scare you? Why did you pull away from me?'

Her eyes fell. What answer could she give, that would satisfy him? 'I thought I'd be leaving soon——' She stopped in the middle of the sentence. Her throat was too tight to let a word pass.

'But now you're not going.'

'No.' It was only a breath.

'So where does that leave us, Whitney?'

She licked dry lips, and looked up at him, and heard herself whisper, 'I want you so very much, Max——'

Some of the strain seemed to go out of him. He pulled her close against him, and she huddled there, absorbing the warmth of his body as she had never expected to be able to again. What difference did some problematic future make, she asked herself a little dizzily, when they could have today?

She raised her face, and when he kissed her she closed her eyes and let herself drift off into a world where there were no such things as concerns for tomorrow, or difficult questions to be answered. There was only today, and the perfect pleasure of Max's arms holding her, Max's mouth caressing her, Max's husky voice telling her how beautiful she was.

I know it will hurt some day, she thought. Loving someone always hurts, one way or another. But at least along with that hurt I shall have the beautiful memories to hug close to me. I shall always know that for a while, in his own way, Max cared for me—— He must care for me, she thought. He came back to me——

'Please,' she whispered. 'Max, make love to me now.'

For a moment, she thought that he hadn't heard. Then he said, 'I think we should talk this out first.'

But I don't want to talk, she thought. I only want to feel. I don't want reason and logic to interfere just now; it might make me think of the future.

She arched her back and pressed her body against him, and let her hands wander through his hair, over his muscled shoulders, down across his back. She kissed him, and let her tongue gently tease, enjoying the taste of him.

Max groaned. 'You're a dangerous woman,' he said.

'Whose fault is that?' She gave him no chance to answer. She was using every trick he had taught her, to break down this unexpected resistance. But in the back of her mind was a nagging question; why was he holding out? Why did he not want to make love to her? What was it that he thought they must talk about?

Making love doesn't solve anything, she told herself. But right now, she needed the reassurance that only physical closeness could give her. Later, there would be time for talk.

'I can't hold out against you,' he murmured, and her questions vanished, swallowed in the sheer delight of his possession. There was no time to question, then, in the urgency of their lovemaking. Every nerve, every cell in her body was thrilling to his touch.

Oh, Max, how much I love you, she thought, and then she could not even think, and the only thing she knew was that this was the most astounding moment of her life, and that all the pleasure she had known with him before was a mere shadow of this supreme joy...

After a while, Max said, 'Now that I have your full attention...' His voice was husky with the aftermath of passion, and he was drawing idle patterns on her skin with a gentle fingertip. 'Did you mean what you said a few minutes ago?'

Every muscle in her body tensed. 'What did I say?' she asked flatly.

Max didn't answer. He was too busy nibbling at her earlobe.

She was trying frantically to remember what she might have said. It didn't sound as if it had bothered him— whatever it was—and yet she was afraid to trust.

'Whitney,' he said, and he was suddenly sober. 'Do the other women that I've known bother you?'

Not any more than a terminal illness would, she thought. The abstract wanderings of his fingers was beginning to torment her. She caught his hand, and tried to keep her voice light. 'Not really. I didn't think you could have learned all that from reading a book.'

'I didn't,' he said. 'And you would probably be shocked to find out how much of it I learned from you.'

She ignored that one. She didn't believe it, anyway, and there was no point in asking to be hurt.

'I talked to Ross this week,' he went on. 'He thinks you're very unhappy in Kansas City. Are you?'

'Not now. I like the idea of having a store of my own.' She didn't like the turn this conversation was taking; she snuggled against him. 'Why so serious?' she asked. 'Let's just enjoy being together, Max.'

'You aren't going to change the subject. I've been seduced once today; now we're going to talk.' He sounded as if he meant it.

'You're behaving like water-torture again,' she complained.

'I know. Be warned, Whitney. I don't give up. What did I do that scared you so?'

'You didn't scare me, Max,' she whispered. 'I frightened myself, that's all.'

She tried to slide out of bed, but Max's arm was like a chain holding her fast.

'I only want a drink of water,' she protested.

'Later.'

He was behaving oddly, she thought. There was nothing left of the uncertainty that she had felt earlier. Just what had caused this sudden change? 'Max,' she demanded suddenly, 'what exactly did I say a little while ago?'

He raised his head and smiled down at her. 'You told me that you loved me.'

'Oh.' For a split second, she was terrified. Of all the idiotic things to do, Whitney, she lectured herself. All your intelligent ideas of how you could have Max if you could only learn to play by the rules, and then you go and do this!

She wouldn't look at him. His breath was disturbingly warm against her cheek. 'Don't women always say that?' she asked.

'It's been my experience,' he mused, 'that you say only what you mean when you're in bed.'

'It has?' she asked hesitantly. Then she gathered her poise, and said, 'Well, it would be no wonder if I did say it. You should have known better.'

Max's eyebrows arched. 'What does that mean?'

'If you feed a starving puppy, you end up with a devoted dog at your heels. You should have known that if you paid any attention to me——' Her voice started to crack.

'Well, I certainly don't want a puppy following me about,' Max interrupted. 'I want a woman walking by my side.'

'You do?' she asked uncertainly.

'That's right. I was miserable in Detroit this week, without you.'

'Me, too,' she admitted.

'But if you're not happy in Kansas City, Whitney, I'll move. Ross still wants me to work for him.'

'But you hate travelling.'

'I'd do it—if I can come home to you.'

He meant it, too. It was obvious in the tone of his voice. Whitney turned her head and let the pillowcase blot up the sudden tears.

But he had seen. 'Are you crying, for heaven's sake?'

'No,' Whitney said, with dignity. 'I got a speck of soot in my eye, and I'm washing it out.'

'Good. I'd hate to think that I made you cry. Now, what about the job?'

She shook her head. 'It's not for you,' she said. 'That job would mean that you'd be on the road most of the time. We wouldn't be together anyway.'

'Do you know that's the first time you've said that it might be important to you—for us to be together?'

'It is,' she whispered. 'It's very important——' Her voice trailed off to a mere whisper. 'I'll stay here in Kansas City, Max, as long as you want me to. It's no sacrifice, really. I like the store, and——'

'And what if you didn't like the store?'

She hesitated, for one long instant, and then told the truth. 'It wouldn't matter. You're more important than the store,' she confessed, in an unsteady whisper.

He buried his face against her neck, his breath warm against the soft skin. 'Then you did mean it when you said you loved me?'

'Yes.' She caught herself, too late. 'But it might not be true,' she pointed out primly. 'I might have convinced myself of it only because you were kind to me.'

'I'm not looking for a way out, Whitney. Are you?'

She shook her head.

His fingers had found her ribs and were counting them. It tickled, and Whitney wriggled a little.

'And you're really prepared to stay in Kansas City for as long as I want you to?' he asked idly.

'Yes.'

'What if I decide next week that I'm tired of you? You'll go away quietly and without fuss?'

The calm, almost cold question sent shivers down Whitney's spine. Horror choked her. Just a moment ago, she had thought that he meant they had a future. She swallowed hard. 'Yes,' she said. 'If that's what you want, Max.'

'I'll just bet you would, too,' Max mused. 'You'd retreat into a cave somewhere and never say a harsh word about me. And what about the alternative, Whitney? What if you get tired of me, and Kansas City, and the store, before I get tired of you?'

'I don't think I could get tired of you, Max,' she admitted warily.

'Ah,' he said, and there was satisfaction in his tone. 'Then you'd better get on the phone to Ross and tell him that you're permanently settled. Because I don't expect to be asking you to leave.'

'Shall I call him right now?'

He looked down at her through narrowed eyelids. 'No, I think it would be safe to wait till tomorrow,' he growled. With a swift movement, he pulled the blankets back. The rush of cool air against her heated skin made Whitney gasp. 'Come on, woman,' he said. 'Out of that bed, lazybones! We have places to go to and things to do.'

Whitney tugged the blankets out of his grasp. 'Tell me where, first.'

'No. I'm in charge of this expedition. Come on.'

'Why? What's so important that I have to get up right now?'

'You're not going to co-operate till I tell you, are you?'

'No.' She piled the pillows up against the head of the bed, and leaned against them. She tried to spread the blanket out evenly, but since she was still under it, the wrinkles refused to disappear.

'I've had a sudden urge to go down to the Plaza for a carriage ride.'

'At this hour? Max, you're crazy!'

'Only about you.'

There was a warm little glow around her heart. 'Why a carriage ride? Are you that fond of horses?'

'Not exactly.'

'Then why?'

'Because I don't want my children to be told that I proposed to their mother in bed, that's why. It wouldn't be a very good example for them.'

Whitney blinked. 'Proposed?' she said weakly.

'Yes. As in, will you marry me. What kind of guy do you think I am, anyway? Is it that much of a shock?'

'Yes, it is. And yes, I will.'

He shook his head. 'You can't accept yet. I haven't officially proposed, and I won't till you get out of bed.'

'Do you really mean it, Max? You're not the marrying kind.'

He settled himself against the pillows next to her, and drew the blanket up around them both. 'I suspect that I'll be a good many years living down all the idiotic things I've said,' he said.

Whitney nodded and put her head down on his shoulder.

'What you're really asking is whether I can let the other women go by, isn't it?'

'I suppose it is.'

'Because old habits die hard.' He sounded a little unhappy. 'But you see, my dear, I've looked for a long time. And I'm as sure right now as it is humanly possible to be that my looking is over. I love you, Whitney, and I'm not fool enough to take any risks with that.'

'You never said anything about loving me,' she murmured.

'No. If I had, when I first knew how I felt about you, you would have run the mile in the world's record time.'

She smiled, a little.

Max's arms tightened around her. 'You scared me to death,' he said unsteadily. 'At first I was sure that you

were healing, that it was only a matter of time until you
were ready to take a chance again. But whenever the
subject of your leaving came up, you seemed eager to
get away from Kansas City—or from me, I didn't know
which. You pulled away from me like a frightened doe
Whitney.'

'I was afraid that you were anxious for me to go,' she
confessed. 'I didn't want you to tell me it was
over——'

'And so you ended it yourself.'

She nodded.

'And every day, I was falling a little harder for you,'
he mused. 'I think the night I called you in Chicago
and lay there all night just listening to you sleep, was
when I first realised how precious you were becoming
to me.'

'Was it worth the phone bill?'

'Sure. But it wasn't as nice as sleeping next to you
and holding you in my arms.' He toyed with a strand of
her hair. 'Honey, I don't know how to convince you that
I'm not like Charles. You are all that I want—all that I
need.'

'All that my heart desires,' she said softly.

'That's right. If you can only put your trust in me
Whitney, I promise that I'll never betray you. Someday
perhaps you can forget how badly Charles hurt
you——'

'Charles who?' she asked. 'Why did you bring that
report up here tonight?'

'Because I couldn't stay away,' he said, unsteadily
'Does that make you happy?'

She nodded. 'Max, darling——' Her fingers wandered over his chest and twirled the dark hair into little
curls.

'Why is it that I'm suspicious of that tone of voice?

'Do you suppose the horse and carriage could wait
till later?'

'How much later?'

Her hand slipped to the back of his neck, and pulled him down to her. 'Much, much later,' she whispered, and kissed him. It was long, and soft, and trusting.

'I think,' Max said unsteadily, 'that they'll probably wait for us for ever.'

Harlequin American Romance

**Romances that go one step farther . . .
American Romance**

Realistic stories involving people you can relate to and care about.

Compelling relationships between the mature men and women of today's world.

Romances that capture the core of genuine emotions between a man and a woman.

Join us each month for four new titles wherever paperback books are sold.
Enter the world of American Romance.

Amro-1

Harlequin Superromance

Here are the longer, more involving stories you have been waiting for...Superromance.

Modern, believable novels of love, full of the complex joys and heartaches of real people.

Intriguing conflicts based on today's constantly changing life-styles.

Four new titles every month.
Available wherever paperbacks are sold.

SUPER-1

ATTRACTIVE, SPACE SAVING BOOK RACK

Display your most prized novels on this handsome and sturdy book rack. The hand-rubbed walnut finish will blend into your library decor with quiet elegance, providing a practical organizer for your favorite hard-or soft-covered books.

Only $9.95

Approximately 16" x 8" when assembled

Assembles in seconds!

To order, rush your name, address and zip code, along with a check or money order for $10.70* ($9.95 plus 75¢ postage and handling) payable to *Harlequin Reader Service*:

Harlequin Reader Service
Book Rack Offer
901 Fuhrmann Blvd.
P.O. Box 1396
Buffalo, NY 14269-1396

Offer not available in Canada.

BKR-1A

*New York and Iowa residents add appropriate sales tax.

Coming Next Month

1151 ALWAYS LOVE Emma Darcy
After four years of silent waiting, Genevra is about to try to find out why Luke
Stanford never returned to her from Australia. Then Christian Nemo comes
into her life—a man so like Luke it sends her into an emotional turmoil!

1152 VILLAIN OF THE PIECE Catherine George
It's unfortunate that the only help available to Lucy and her young son is from
Joss Woodbridge—the man who had ruined her life once already. However
generous, he's the last man she wants to turn to....

1153 AN EXPERT TEACHER Penny Jordan
Her return for her brother's wedding reinforces all Gemma's feelings of being
a misfit in her parents' wealthy world. And after seeing the older,
sophisticated Luke she'd unwittingly rejected as a teenager, Gemma is faced
with a commitment she's not quite sure she can make.

1154 THE LOVING GAMBLE Flora Kidd
Scottish designer Rachel Dow and investment analyst Ross Fraser meet in the
United States, have a whirlwind romance and marry. Only back in Scotland
does Rachel begin to suspect that Ross's motives aren't as simple as she'd
imagined—and his answers to her questions are unconvincing.

1155 A FLOOD OF SWEET FIRE Sandra Marton
Everything's working well, Blair thinks as she flies to Italy pretending to be
Meryl Desmond. Her young socialite boss has reasons to avoid the press. But
outside Rome airport she suddenly finds herself victim of a kidnap attempt
and captive of a mysterious man called Rhys Hunter....

1156 ILLUSION OF PARADISE Joanna Mansell
Jay Challoner never gave interviews, so journalist Charlie resorts to rather
devious methods to spend some time with him. Disappointed when he has to
rush off to Ecuador, she gets the shock of her life when he agrees to take her
with him!

1157 THE BITTER TASTE OF LOVE Lilian Peake
Used to advising other people, when it comes to her own life Jemma finds
things aren't so simple. She's swept into a whirlwind marriage and loves her
artistic husband. But she doesn't always understand him—or his explanations
about Joanna....

1158 HOT PURSUIT Karen van der Zee
Henk Hofstra pursues Natasha with a single-mindedness that makes her
question her cynical vow never to get involved with a man again. Does his
determination and their shared Dutch background mean she can really trust
him?

Available in March wherever paperback books are sold, or through
Harlequin Reader Service:

In the U.S.
901 Fuhrmann Blvd.
P.O. Box 1397
Buffalo, N.Y. 14240-1397

In Canada
P.O. Box 603
Fort Erie, Ontario
L2A 5X3

Harlequin Intrigue

Two exciting new stories each month.

Each title mixes a contemporary, sophisticated romance with the surprising twists and turns of a puzzler...romance with "something more."

Because romance can be quite an adventure.

Romance, Suspense and Adventure

Patricia Matthews, "America's First Lady of Romance," will delight her fans with these spellbinding sagas of passion and romance, glamour and intrigue.

Thursday and the Lady	$4.50	☐
A story of a proud and passionate love set during America's most unforgettable era—as suffragettes waged their struggle for the vote, the gold rush spurred glorious optimism and the Civil War loomed on the horizon.		
Mirrors	$4.50	☐
Intrigue, passion and murder surround a young woman when she learns that she is to inherit an enormous family fortune.		
Enchanted	$3.95	☐
Caught in the steamy heat of America's New South, a young woman finds herself torn between two brothers—she yearns for one but a dark, foreboding secret binds her to the other.		
Oasis	$4.50	☐
A spellbinding story chronicling the lives of the movie stars, politicians and rock celebrities who converge at the world-famous addiction clinic in Oasis.		

Total Amount	$
Plus 75¢ Postage	.75
Payment enclosed	

Please send a check or money order payable to Worldwide Library.

In U.S.A.	In Canada
Worldwide Library	Worldwide Library
901 Fuhrmann Blvd.	P.O. Box 609
Box 1325	Fort Erie, Ontario
Buffalo, NY 14269-1325	L2A 5X3

Please Print

Name: _____

Address: _____

City: _____

State/Prov: _____

Zip/Postal Code: _____

 WORLDWIDE LIBRARY